"You're not like any man I've ever tried to seduce, Dallas Cole."

"Is that good or bad?"

She cocked her head, a smile flirting with her kiss-stung lips. "Both."

"In case it's not clear, I do want you."

She stepped closer until she pressed against him. "I know."

She was damn near impossible to resist, but he made himself ease her away. "We have to trust each other."

"Yes," she agreed.

"And sex complicates things."

"It does."

"It would be easy to let myself get caught up in you, as a way of forgetting..."

"Comfort sex."

"Yes." He stole a look at her. "I don't want there to be any doubts between us. I don't want you to ever feel used."

"A little late for that," she said in a wry tone, and he realized she was revealing more about her past than perhaps she meant to.

BLUE RIDGE RICOCHET

—

Paula Graves

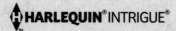

HARLEQUIN® INTRIGUE®

For my readers. Thank you for all your support.
I couldn't live this dream without you.

Recycling programs
for this product may
not exist in your area.

ISBN-13: 978-0-373-74939-3

Blue Ridge Ricochet

Copyright © 2016 by Paula Graves

Printed in U.S.A.

Paula Graves, an Alabama native, wrote her first book at the age of six. A voracious reader, Paula loves books that pair tantalizing mystery with compelling romance. When she's not reading or writing, she works as a creative director for a Birmingham advertising agency and spends time with her family and friends. Paula invites readers to visit her website, paulagraves.com.

Books by Paula Graves

Harlequin Intrigue

The Gates: Most Wanted

Smoky Mountain Setup
Blue Ridge Ricochet

The Gates

Dead Man's Curve
Crybaby Falls
Boneyard Ridge
Deception Lake
Killshadow Road
Two Souls Hollow

Bitterwood P.D.

Murder in the Smokies
The Smoky Mountain Mist
Smoky Ridge Curse
Blood on Copperhead Trail
The Secret of Cherokee Cove
The Legend of Smuggler's Cave

Visit the Author Profile page at Harlequin.com for more titles.

CAST OF CHARACTERS

Nicki Jamison—Deep undercover as a diner fry cook in a tiny mountain town, Nicki is close to uncovering the identity of the leader of the Blue Ridge Infantry. The last thing she needs to deal with is the fugitive who has just landed in her lap.

Dallas Cole—Helping an associate in trouble has sent the FBI graphic designer running for his life. Trusting anyone is sheer folly, but the beautiful brunette who scrapes him up from an icy road and takes him home to recuperate makes him want to believe he's not completely alone.

Alexander Quinn—The former CIA agent who runs The Gates knows he's put Nicki in grave danger. Just how deep will he let her go on her own?

The Blue Ridge Infantry—The dangerous militia group took Dallas captive and pumped him for information he didn't have. Now that he's escaped, are they still looking for him? Or have they turned their attention to the curious fry cook asking questions about them?

Philip Crandall—The FBI assistant director was the last person Dallas talked to before the Blue Ridge Infantry grabbed him. Is Crandall one of the BRI's contacts inside the FBI?

Trevor Colley—Nicki's boss at the diner is suspicious about the friends she's made among members of the Blue Ridge Infantry.

Del McClintock—The BRI member doesn't hide his interest in Nicki. Could he be her ticket to the militia's inner circle?

John Bartholomew—The mystery man acts as a go-between for Nicki and Quinn. But can he be trusted when everything goes wrong?

Chapter One

Sleet rattled against the windshield, a staccato counterpoint to the rhythmic *swish-swish* of the windshield wipers. Outside, night had fallen in inky finality, as if it planned to stay awhile, the Jeep's headlights the only illumination as far as the eye could see.

Nicolette Jamison forced herself out of a weary slouch behind the steering wheel and concentrated on the curving mountain road revealed in her headlights, well aware of the treachery that lay ahead for a careless driver. The switchbacks and drop-offs in the Blue Ridge Mountains could be deadly if you weren't paying attention. Not to mention the occasional reckless deer or coyote—

"Son of a—!"

The man loomed in the Jeep's headlights as suddenly as if the swirling mist had conjured him up, a tall, lean phantom of a man who turned slowly to face the headlights as she hit the brakes and prayed she wouldn't go into a skid this dangerously close to a steep drop-off.

The Jeep's wheels grabbed the blacktop and hung on, the vehicle shimmying to a stop just a yard away from the apparition gazing back at her through the windshield. For a second, she had a strange sense of recognition, as if she knew him, though she was pretty sure she didn't.

Then his eyes fluttered closed and he dropped out of sight.

Nicki's heart stuttered like a snare drum against her rib cage as she stared at the misty void where, seconds earlier, she'd seen the staring man.

Ghost, her inner twelve-year-old intoned, sending her heart rate soaring steeply for a few seconds before her grown-up side took charge. She checked the rearview mirror for coming traffic, saw only the faint red glow of her own taillights, and put the car in Reverse, backing up carefully until she could see what the front of the Jeep had concealed—a man lying in a crumpled heap in the center of the narrow two-lane road.

She pulled the Jeep to the shoulder on the mountain side of the road and parked, engaging her hazard lights and trying to calm her rattled nerves. The man could be hurt.

Or it could be a trick. Maybe she should call the sheriff's department and let them handle things.

Except…

Buck up, Nicki. This is the life you chose.

Her weapons of choice these days were pepper spray and sheer nerve, and so far, she'd survived on their one-two punch. But something about the man lying crumpled on the road in front of her made her nerve waver. There was still something eerily familiar about him, a memory tugging at the back of her mind, trying to make itself known.

Holding the pepper-spray canister out in front of her, she approached the man, easing into a crouch just beyond reach. She shifted position so that the glow from the Jeep's headlights fell across the man's face.

He was younger than she'd thought, in his midthirties at most. His pallor, combined with the sunken cheeks and shadowed eyes that came with illness, had made him look older. He was still breathing, she saw with relief.

"Mister?"

He stirred at the sound of her voice, his eyelids flickering open to half-mast, then drifting shut again. He muttered something that sounded like a string of numbers, but she couldn't quite make them out.

Gingerly, she reached out to check his pulse. Fast but steady and stronger than she'd anticipated. "Where are you hurt?"

He murmured numbers again. She made out a two and a four before he stopped.

She pulled her cell phone from the pocket of her jeans and tried to dial 911, then realized she didn't have any reception. "Damn it." She pocketed the phone and stared at him for a second, considering her options. Leaving him here in the road wasn't an option. And without cell phone reception, calling for help wasn't an option, either. The temperature was right at the freezing mark, and his skin was cold to the touch, which suggested he might already be suffering from exposure.

He was breathing. He was at least semiconscious. His heart rate was a little fast but steady as a rock, so he didn't seem likely to go into cardiac arrest anytime soon. And he'd definitely been mobile before he collapsed in front of her vehicle, so he didn't seem to have any spinal issues.

She had to get him warm, and the Jeep was the best bet. The old Wrangler had seen better days, but its heater still worked.

But how was she supposed to haul this man into her Jeep?

"Mister, think you can stay with me long enough for me to get you to my car?"

He opened his eyes, looking straight at her, and that niggle of recognition returned. "Who're you?"

"My name's Nicki. What's yours?"

"Dallas."

For a brief second, she wondered if he'd misunderstood her question. Then the memory that had been flickering in and out of the back of her mind popped to the front, and she sat back on her heels, almost toppling over.

Dallas. As in Dallas Cole, missing for almost three weeks now and presumed by most people as either dead and buried somewhere in the Blue Ridge Mountains or wintering somewhere on the coast of Mexico, a cerveza in hand and a pretty girl by his side.

The last place she'd figured on running into the missing FBI employee was on Bellwether Road in the middle of Dudley County, Virginia.

Now she could see the resemblance between the man lying in the road in front of her and the missing man whose disappearance had caused a stir all the way from Washington, DC, to the little town of Purgatory, Tennessee, where a man named Alexander Quinn ran a security agency called The Gates.

"Oh, hell," she murmured.

A frown furrowed his brow. "Where am I?"

"Ever heard of River's End, Virginia?"

His voice rasped as he answered. "No."

"Not surprising."

He struggled to sit up. Not quite sure she could trust him yet, she let him do so without her help, her gaze sweeping over him in search of injuries. She spotted healing bruises dotting his jawline and the evidence of old blood spotting the front of his grimy gray shirt, but no sign of recent injuries.

Mostly, he looked exhausted and cold, and while she was no doctor, she could help him out with those two ailments. "Think you can stand?"

He pulled his legs up and gave a push with his arms, wincing as his left arm gave out and he landed on his backside. "Something's wrong with my shoulder."

Could be a trick, her wary mind warned, but she ignored it, following the demands of her compassionate heart. He couldn't fake the unmistakable look of ill health. Something had happened to this man, no matter what crimes had led him to this place, and the least she could do was get him somewhere warm and dry before feds came swarming into River's End.

She started to reach for him, planning to help him to his feet, when her last thought finally penetrated her brain.

She pulled back, staring at him with alarm.

"What's wrong?" he asked, slanting her a suspicious look.

"Nothing," she lied, even as her mind started scrambling for a solution to her unexpected dilemma. There was no way she could leave him to fend for himself out here in the sleet. There was supposed to be snow before midnight, and the temps were going to plunge into the midtwenties before morning. Dressed as he was, without even a coat to ward off the chill, he'd never survive the night.

But if she took him to the hospital in Bristol...

She couldn't. They'd call the FBI, who'd want to talk to her. There'd be a lot of terribly inconvenient questions and all her work for the past few months would be out the window.

Or worse.

But how to explain that to the hypothermic, battered man sitting in the road in front of her?

"Look, I tried calling 911—"

"No." His gaze snapped up sharply, catching her off guard.

"No?"

"I don't need medical help." His lips pressed to a thin line. "I'm okay. I just need to get warm."

Well, she thought, *that wasn't exactly a comforting reaction.*

"Are you sure?" Not that she wanted to contact authorities any more than he did, but his reluctance didn't exactly fit the picture of a man wrongly accused, did it?

Maybe that was good, though, considering the dangerous game she was playing herself. Dealing with bad guys was less complicated than dealing with good ones, she'd discovered. Their motives

easier to glean and usually involved one sin
or another. Greed, gluttony, lust, hate—oh, yeah,
she definitely knew how to deal with sinners.

Saints, on the other hand, were a cipher.

"Let's get you out of the cold, Dallas." She
pushed aside questions of his particular motives. There'd be time to figure him out once she
got him back to her cabin, where she could provide the basic comforts anyone in his condition
needed, whether sinner or saint.

Avoiding his bad shoulder, she pulled his right
arm around her shoulder and helped him to his
feet. He stumbled a little as they made their way
across the slickening blacktop to the Jeep, but she
settled him in the passenger seat with little fuss
and watched with bemusement as he fumbled the
seat belt into place. Sinner or not, he apparently
took seat belt safety seriously.

She circled around, slid behind the Jeep's steer-
ing wheel and cranked the engine. Next to her,
Dallas sighed audibly as heat blasted from the
Jeep's vents.

"Good?" she asked, easing back onto the road.

"Heaven," he murmured through chattering
teeth.

He couldn't have been out in the elements for
long, she realized as his shivering began to ease
before they'd gone more than a mile down the
road. So where the hell had he come from?

"Should I be worrying about pursuit?" she asked.

His gaze slanted toward her. "Pursuit?"

"Anybody after you?"

He didn't answer at first. She didn't push, too busy dealing with the steady buildup of icy precipitation forming on the mountain road. Thank God she didn't have much farther to travel. The little cabin she called home was only a quarter mile down the road. They'd be there before the snow started.

"There might be," he answered finally as she slowed into the turn down the gravel road that ended at her cabin.

"Are they nearby?"

"Probably," he answered.

Great. Just great.

"What did you do?" She glanced his way.

His mouth crooked in the corner. "Because people in trouble usually got there under their own steam?"

She shrugged. "Usually."

"I broke a rule. I thought it was for a good reason, but as usual, the rules are there for a reason."

He was beginning to sound more like a saint than a sinner. "What kind of rule?"

"I skipped steps I should have taken," he said obliquely.

But she knew enough about his situation to

...w exactly what he was talking about, even if ...he didn't let on. "That's cryptic."

He smiled. "Yes."

So. He didn't trust her any more than she trusted him. Fair enough. She was in no position to quibble.

"Well, how about we don't worry about rules and secrets, and just get you somewhere warm and dry. Think you could handle something to eat?"

"Yes," he said with an eagerness that made her glance his way again. He met her gaze with a quick glance, his lips quirking again. "Sorry. I've missed a meal or three."

When he smiled, he was almost good-looking even with his sunken eyes and hollow cheeks, something she hadn't expected. The only photo she'd seen of him had been his driver's license photo. Nobody ever looked good in their driver's license photos.

Dallas Cole, she suspected, would clean up nicely.

Down, girl. He's not date material, and you've sworn off men, remember? Saints or sinners, they're nothing but trouble.

She pulled the Jeep under the carport connected to her cabin and cut the engine. "Sure you don't want me to call paramedics?"

His eyes were closed, his head resting against

the back of the seat. When he turned his face toward her, his eyes opened slowly to meet hers in the gloom. "I just need to rest a little while. Then I'll get out of your hair."

The full impact of what she was doing hit her as she got out of the Jeep and locked the door behind her. Had she lost her mind, taking in a stranger wanted by the FBI? Even Alexander Quinn, a man who prided himself on his ability to read people, wasn't sure what side Dallas Cole had chosen. For all she knew, this might be a test of her loyalty to the Blue Ridge Infantry.

She had to tread carefully. Everything she'd worked for over the past few months was at stake.

Dallas stumbled on his way to the door, flashing her a grimace of a smile as she grabbed his arm and kept him from face-planting in the gravel between the Jeep and her kitchen door. "I'm usually steadier on my feet."

"How long has it been since you ate anything?"

"Not counting roots and berries?" he asked with a lopsided smile, leaning against the side of her house while she unlocked the door.

"Yeah, not counting those." She opened the door and helped him up the two shallow steps into the kitchen.

Inside, the cabin was blessedly warm and familiar, driving away some of Nicki's tension. Dallas Cole didn't seem to be faking his weakness, and she was finally back in her own comfort zone. She knew where the knives were kept and where to find her Remington 870 pump-action shotgun and ammo.

And there was the satellite phone hidden under the mattress of her bed that would get Alexander Quinn on the line in a second. He might be two and a half hours away in Purgatory, Tennessee, but he had eyes and ears all over the hills. She knew from experience.

"How much snow do you think we'll get?" Dallas asked as she flicked the switch on the wall, flooding the kitchen with light. He squinted at her, as if it had been a while since his eyes had been accustomed to so much light.

"I guess you haven't heard a forecast in a few days?" She crossed to the stove and grabbed one of the saucepans hanging over the range. "We'll get an inch or two, maybe. It'll probably be melted off by tomorrow afternoon."

"Glad to be out of it." He nodded toward the small kitchen nook table. "May I?"

Polite, she thought. Though she'd met a few well-mannered devils in her day who'd give you the shaft and thank you for it. "Sit. I'll see what's in the pantry."

He groaned a little as he sat, and she wondered how many injuries he had hidden beneath his grimy clothes. "Thank you. I'm not sure how I'll be able to repay you for your kindness."

His accent was subtle but there, the hint of a mountain twang not unlike her own Tennessee accent. She'd done little more than glance over the information Quinn's mystery operative had left for her at the dead drop a few weeks earlier before she'd destroyed it, not exactly expecting Dallas Cole to show up in the middle of River's End. But there'd been something about a hometown in eastern Kentucky—

"No repayment necessary." She looked through the cans in her pantry. "Chicken and vegetable sound okay?"

"Sounds like heaven."

As she heated the soup, she searched her brain for any other details she could remember from the dossier on Dallas Cole. His job at the FBI wasn't exactly what she might have expected— that much she remembered. She wasn't dealing with a special agent or a forensic science whiz.

No, he was a graphic designer with the Bureau's public affairs office.

How on earth had an artist gotten himself crossways with the Blue Ridge Infantry?

HE HAD NO idea what to do next, so he did nothing. Nothing but sit and bask in the warmth of this tiny kitchen and watch a blue-eyed brunette with killer curves heating a can of chicken soup on an ancient gas range.

Nicki, she'd said. Short for Nicole?

"This is a nice place," he said, mostly to end the silence. Over the past three weeks, silence had become his enemy, an auditory void in which his deepest fears had held sway.

She glanced toward him. "Compared to what?"

Her blunt tone made his lips twitch with unaccustomed humor. He hadn't had a lot to laugh about recently. "I've been worse places."

"Haven't we all?" She pulled a couple of stoneware bowls from a nearby cabinet and put them on the counter by the stove. "You in the mood for a little or a lot?"

His stomach seemed to be turning eager flips, but his brain kicked in with a stern warning. The last thing he wanted to do in front of a pretty girl like Nicki was throw up. "Let's start with a little."

She slanted a curious look his way but put a bowl half-full of steaming soup on the table in front of him. "Careful. It's hot." She fetched a spoon and put it by the bowl.

He blew on a spoonful of the soup and took a sip. The savory broth tasted like heaven in a spoon.

Nicki took the seat across from him, not looking at him as she started eating her own bowl of soup.

Prickles of suspicion played at the back of his neck. Why wasn't she looking at him?

"Just you here?" he asked.

Her gaze snapped up to meet his, and he realized how shady the question probably seemed.

Her green-eyed gaze leveled with his. "Me and my Remington 870."

He smiled at that. "Message received."

"Sorry. That was a tad rude, wasn't it?" One corner of her lips tilted upward.

"Probably earned it with that badly phrased question." He fell silent and concentrated on eating his soup as slowly as his ravening hunger would allow. His stomach felt unsettled but the food was staying down, at least for the time being.

He needed food and rest, in that order. Because once he left this cabin, he wasn't sure when he'd get much of either again.

"How did you end up out there in the woods?"

The question he'd been waiting for ever since she'd stopped to help. "It's a long story."

"And you don't want to tell it?" In her voice, he heard a surprising thread of sympathy. He looked up and saw her sharp eyes watching him with understanding.

"Not at the present," he admitted.

"Okay." She turned her attention back to her soup.

That was easy.

Too easy.

He didn't know how to deal with someone who didn't seem to want—or need—one damn thing from him. Especially after the ordeal of the past few weeks. He didn't know how to relax anymore, how to sit quietly and eat a bowl of soup without waiting for the next blow, the next trick.

He knew his name was Dallas Logan Cole. He was thirty-three years old and had spent the first eighteen years of his life in Kentucky coal country, trying like hell to get out before he was stuck there for the rest of his sorry life. He was a good artist and an even better designer, and he'd spent the bulk of his college years trying to leave behind the last vestiges of his mountain upbringing so he could start a whole new life.

And here he was, back in the hills, running for his life again. How the hell had he let this happen?

"I guess those are the only clothes you have?"

He looked down at his grimy shirt and jeans. They weren't the clothes he'd been wearing when a group of men in pickup trucks had run his car off the road a few miles north of Ruckersville, Virginia. The wreck had left him a little woozy and helpless to fight the four burly mountain men who'd hauled him into one of the trucks and driven him into the hills. They'd stripped him out of his suit and made him dress in the middle of the woods in the frigid cold while they watched with hawk-sharp eyes for any sign of rebellion.

Rebellion, he'd later learned, was the quickest way to earn a little extra pain.

"It's all I have," he said, swallowing enough humiliating memories to last a lifetime. "Don't suppose you have anything my size?"

Her lips quirked again, triggering a pair of dimples in her cheeks. "Not on purpose. I can wash those for you, though."

"I'd appreciate that." He was finally warm, he realized with some surprise. Not a shiver in sight. He'd begun to wonder if he'd ever feel truly warm again.

She picked up his empty bowl and took it to the sink. "The bathroom's down the hall to the right. Leave your clothes in the hall and I'll put them on to wash."

"And then what?"

She turned as if surprised by the question. "And then we go to bed."

Chapter Two

Dallas gave Nicki an odd look. "To bed?"

She looked up quickly, realizing what she'd just said, and couldn't hold back a grin. "Not together, big guy."

He smiled back. "Yeah, I didn't figure you meant it that way. But this cabin's not very big. Do you even have a second bedroom?"

"No," she admitted. "But I have a sofa. And extra blankets. So go on and take a shower. Or a bath, if you like. The tub's pretty big." She bit back a smile at the thought of Dallas Cole folding his lanky body into her tub.

"Still the problem of clothes. Or the lack thereof."

"I probably have some sweats around here somewhere. I borrowed them from my cousin the last time I stayed at his place." Anson was only a couple of inches taller than Dallas, so surely his old sweatpants would fit him well enough. "Go get cleaned up. And let me know if you find any wounds you need treated."

The wary look he shot her way sent a prickle of unease racing up her neck. He was one more person who didn't quite trust her version of the truth.

And why should he? Why should anyone? She was lying through her teeth about what she was doing in River's End, wasn't she?

There'd been a time, not so long ago, when lying came as naturally to her as breathing. Life was one big story to be told the way she wanted it to happen, and inconvenient truths were discarded like yesterday's trash.

But she'd learned the hard way that the truth always came out, and usually at the worst possible time. She just hoped the truth about her assignment here in River's End didn't come out until she was somewhere safe and far, far away.

DALLAS LET THE shower run as hot as he dared and stood under the needling spray until he couldn't stand on his trembling legs another minute.

Wrapping a towel around his hips, he sat on the closed commode and willed his strength to return. The last thing he wanted to do was face-plant in front of Nicki again. She pitied him enough already.

As the steamy heat of the bathroom dissipated, cooler air washed over his damp skin, raising goose bumps again. He grabbed a second towel from the nearby rack and dried off before he pushed to his feet.

Standing in front of the mirror over the sink, he wiped away the condensation to take his first good look at his physical condition after nearly three weeks of captivity.

He'd lost weight. At least fifteen pounds. Maybe more. The people who'd imprisoned him in the cellar of their mountain cabin had used deprivation to try to break him. Sleep, light, food—all had been withheld in an attempt to get him to tell everything he knew about a man named Cade Landry.

He wondered if Landry was still alive. From what little he'd learned from the men who'd held him captive, getting their hands on Landry was a big damn deal.

But they hadn't gotten any information from him. Maybe they'd thought he was soft because he was nothing but a support staffer at the FBI, working a job that didn't require him to carry a weapon or stay in fighting shape.

They'd been wrong.

Not that he felt anywhere close to fighting shape at the moment. The mirror was merciless, revealing not only his prominent ribs but also the rainbow of bruises and scrapes he'd acquired during his time with the Blue Ridge Infantry.

He made himself turn away from his self-scrutiny and opened the bathroom door. Cold air from the hall assaulted him, and he wrapped the second towel around his shoulders.

"There are clothes on the end of the bed, across the hall." Nicki's voice drifted into the hall from the front room.

"Thanks." He entered the bedroom and found a small stack of clothes at the end of the bed. There was a pair of black sweatpants that wouldn't have fit him three weeks ago but now snugged over his hips as if they'd been made for him. She'd also laid out a couple of oversize football jerseys. He grabbed the darker of the two and shrugged it on. It fit only marginally better.

He dropped to the edge of the bed, tempted to lie down and sleep for a few days. But there was the matter of the pretty brunette down the hall. All the way through his shower, he couldn't stop thinking about what a stroke of fortune it had been to walk into the path of a woman who hadn't asked any inconvenient questions. Who hadn't insisted on calling the police when he asked her not to. What absolute luck.

Problem was, he'd never put much faith in the notion of luck.

Why hadn't she asked him more about who he was and how he'd found himself facedown on a mountain road in the middle of a sleet storm?

He looked around until he found the scuffed oxfords he'd been wearing since he'd been run off the road somewhere north of Ruckersville. The dress shoes looked incongruous with the sweats and jersey, but he didn't like the vulnerability of bare feet at the moment.

Nicki looked up as he entered the living room. She offered a gentle smile that made her look like a goddess, her skin gleaming in the glow of the fire she'd just turned from stoking.

"Thanks for the clothes."

"They fit. Sort of." She stood and dusted her hands on her jeans. They hugged her curves like a lover, sending a rush of desire darting through his belly. He ignored his body's inconvenient reaction, determined to stay focused and on alert.

"I think I've lost weight," he said.

Her eyes narrowed slightly as she moved closer to him. "You seemed pretty hungry earlier."

"You haven't asked me how I got in this condition."

For a second, her faint smile faltered, and he realized he'd struck a nerve. But her smile recovered quickly and she gave an artful shrug. "I didn't want to pry until you were warm and fed. Maybe got some rest, you know? You've clearly been through a lot. I figured you might want to wait to tell me about it until you felt better."

He took a step closer to her, taking advantage

of the difference in their height. "I could be a serial killer for all you know."

She didn't flinch, her smile expanding as his legs began to wobble under him. "I think I could take you. In this condition, anyway."

He reached for the nearest armchair and sat, his legs trembling. The heat of the fire nearby was too tempting to resist; he turned toward the flames, stretching out his hands while slanting a look at his pretty hostess. "You're one of those women who's not afraid of anything?"

"Oh, you've never seen me with a spider," she answered lightly as she pulled her own armchair next to him.

One corner of his mouth lifted. "Now I know how to pay you back for your hospitality. Arachnicide is my specialty. Just give me a rolled-up piece of paper and stand back."

The smile she darted his way made his gut twist unexpectedly. Damn, but she was a good-looking woman, all wavy dark hair and eyes the color of a summer sky. And those jeans and that snug-fitting T-shirt showed off a slim but deliciously curvy body that he hoped would haunt his dreams tonight.

Anything to drive away the nightmares that had tormented him since the truck full of bearded thugs had run him off the road nearly a month ago.

"Is there someone I should call?" She stretched her own small hands toward the fire.

How could he answer that? The truth was, he wasn't sure what to do. The FBI employee he'd been for over a decade demanded that he call the authorities, turn himself in and tell his story. The truth would out.

But the boy from eastern Kentucky knew that sometimes, the truth wasn't enough to keep a man alive. Some of the most evil people in the world could hide behind a badge and the veil of authority. He knew that from experience, including his most recent brush with corruption in the guise of justice.

"I'm not sure," he said finally. "I think maybe sleeping on it is a good idea, if that's okay with you."

Her eyes narrowed slightly at his words, but she just gave a nod and laid her head back against the chair. They sat in silence for a while, tension sharpening the warm air wafting around them.

Did she think his hesitation meant he had something to hide from the authorities? Was she considering calling the cops herself as soon as he went to bed?

It was a chance he'd have to take, because he was almost asleep as it was. If he stayed here much longer, he wasn't sure he could drag himself out of this chair. And no matter how tough or strong she thought she was, he doubted she could haul his weary butt over to the sofa by herself.

"I'll take the sofa," he offered. "No need to run you out of your bed."

She shook her head. "Take the bed. You're the one in bad condition. The sofa sleeps fine, and I'm short enough not to be uncomfortable sleeping on it." She waved her hand toward the pillows and blankets piled up at the end of the sofa. "I'm set for the night."

He looked at her, taking in the guileless expression on her face. He wanted desperately to trust someone, especially someone as pretty as the woman who'd introduced herself as Nicki. But trust didn't come easily to someone like him on the best of days. And good days had been thin on the ground for him for a while now.

"You're remarkably easygoing for someone who just had a stranger crash her life," he said as he pushed to his feet.

She rose with him. "That'll probably change when you're stronger."

"Glad to know you plan to keep me on my toes."

"I've seen you flat on your face. On your toes is definitely the way to go." She nodded toward the hallway. "Go to bed. I'll lock up and we'll see how you feel in the morning."

The walk to the bedroom felt as if he was hiking uphill all the way, but he finally made it to the edge of the bed and sank on the soft mattress, facedown. He would move in just a minute. Crawl under the covers and settle down like a real human being.

It was the last lucid thought he had for a long while.

WHEN SHE CHECKED on Dallas Cole, she found him lying facedown on the bed, angled diagonally across the mattress as if he'd fallen asleep as soon as his body hit the bed.

Good. She needed him to be dead to the world for a little while.

She had somewhere to go.

Bundling up against the dropping temperature outside, she headed east through the woods that butted up to her cabin, going uphill for almost a mile until she reached the small creek that snaked its way down the mountain to join with Bowden Fork south of River's End. At this particular curve of the stream, there was a small natural cave that was only a few feet deep and barely tall enough for Nicki to enter hunched over.

Just inside, a loose stone hid a cavity about eight inches deep into the cave wall. About the size of the mail cubbyhole at the motel where she'd worked a few years ago, the cavity was just big enough to hold a folded-up letter like the one tucked in the pocket of her jeans.

She took a deep breath and tucked the letter into the cavity, then replaced the stone.

Outside the cave, she scanned the woods around her to be certain she was alone. But there was nobody else out there. Only idiots and people with something to hide would be out in this weather.

Next to the cave was a fallen log. She turned the log onto its side until a broken limb about the length of her forearm revealed itself. She propped up the log with a stone to keep it from rolling back over and headed back down the mountain toward her cabin.

She didn't know how often the man she thought of as Agent X passed this way. Sometimes two or more days would go by before she'd see the log back in its original position, her signal that something was waiting for her inside the cave cubbyhole.

But she had a feeling he passed this way daily, just in case she needed his help. At least, she liked to think he did.

It made her feel a little less alone in this dangerous world in which she now operated.

The people she worked with at the diner in town called her a dinosaur because she eschewed so much of the technology they couldn't live without. She owned no computer, though she knew more about how to use them than any of her co-workers and customers would believe. She had a cell phone out of necessity, since power on the mountain could go down so easily, leaving her without phone service, as well. But she turned on the phone only when her landline wasn't work-ing. She had no desire to be instantly reachable, especially when she was on what she'd come to think of as her secret missions.

How on earth had her life come to this? There'd been a time, not very long ago, when nobody who knew her would believe she'd take on a dangerous undercover mission on the side of the good guys.

Not Nicolette Jamison, the wild girl from the Smoky Mountains who'd never met a bad situa-tion she couldn't make worse. Somehow, by the grace of God and a generous utilization of her good looks and native charm, she'd managed to skirt the edge of the law without quite crossing the point of no return, keeping her record clean enough to pass cursory scrutiny.

She'd never pretended to be a saint. Hell, she wasn't one now.

But she knew the difference between trouble and evil. Trouble could lose you a few nights of sleep. Evil would rob you of your life without blinking. And the men she was tangling with these days were about as evil as they came in these parts.

Snow had begun to fall by the time she reached the clearing where her cabin slumbered quietly in the dark. Fat, fluffy flakes started to pile up on her shoulders and dampen the ski cap she'd tugged down to cover her ears. She hurried up the porch steps as quickly as she dared, dodging the spot on the second step that creaked whenever it took any weight, and hurried to the front door, automatically checking the lock to make sure it was still secure.

Still locked up, nice and tight.

She slipped her key into the lock and turned it carefully. The door opened with only the faintest of creaks and closed behind her with an almost imperceptible snick. She engaged the lock and sat in the nearest chair to remove her hiking boots before she padded silently in socked feet down the hallway toward her bedroom.

The door was still open a crack, just as she'd left it. She could just make out Dallas Cole's lean form, still lying diagonally across the bed. She waited a moment until she could make out the steady rise and fall of his breathing before she tiptoed back to the living room and finished undressing for the night.

She slipped on a pair of flannel pajamas she'd found tucked in the bottom of her drawer, a gag gift from her cousin last Christmas inspired by her past visit, when he'd found her sleeping in his bed, dressed in his Atlanta Braves T-shirt and nothing else. The timing had been particularly bad, given that he'd promised his bed to the pretty blonde he had brought home for the night.

Flannel pajamas were about as far from her normal nighttime attire as it got, but she was trying out the straight and narrow these days. Well, straighter and narrower, anyway. No more wandering around in skimpy nighties when strange men were staying the night.

No more strange men staying the night anymore, for that matter. Some undesirable habits deserved to be broken, and her addiction to bad boys was one of them.

She wondered what kind of boy Dallas Cole was. If all she had to go on was the FBI record her boss, Alexander Quinn, had gotten his hands on, she'd say Dallas Cole was about as good a boy as they got. Hardworking, well liked by his colleagues, a go-getter who was looking to move up the ladder at the FBI even though he wasn't a special agent.

What had happened that night three weeks ago when he'd headed south out of Washington, DC, and disappeared without a trace until now?

Did he have a hidden bad-boy side nobody had ever seen?

She had to find out before he was strong enough to give her real trouble.

DALLAS EASED HIS eyes open when he heard Nicki's soft footfalls retreat down the hall. Damn. That had been close.

He'd barely made it back to the bedroom before he heard her key in the front door lock, a tiny clink of metal on metal that he probably wouldn't have noticed if he hadn't been listening for it. If he'd still been asleep, he wouldn't have heard it at all.

But the sound of her leaving had roused him from a deep sleep, leaving his nerves jangling and his mind reeling. He'd dragged himself from bed in time to see her disappear into the woods on the right side of the house, bundled up against the cold.

He'd waited by the window until his legs had given out, then sat in the chair near the fire for almost an hour, going by the clock on the mantel that ticked away the minutes with sharp little clicks of the second hand.

Where the hell had she gone? Did she go to meet someone?

Had she told anyone where to find him?

It didn't matter, he realized as his vigil ticked over to a new hour. He was too tired and weak to make his escape. He had nowhere to go.

Her footsteps on the porch had jolted him from a light doze a few minutes ago. He'd peeked through the narrow gap in the curtains in time to see her easing her way up the wooden porch steps.

He'd made it back to the bed with only seconds to spare, forcing his respiration to a slow, even tempo even though his heart was racing like a rabbit chased by a fox.

He eased over to his back, wincing a little as the bed creaked. He held his breath, waiting for her to return, but after a few minutes, he realized she must have settled down for the night.

He stared at the dark ceiling over his head, his heart still pounding from the rush of adrenaline that had driven him back to bed.

Where had she gone tonight? Who had she seen? What had she said?

Would he live to regret stumbling into her path tonight?

Chapter Three

Frost painted the cabin windows with delicate fronds of ice, lit by the morning sunlight angling through the glass. Outside, snow blanketed the ground and glistened in the trees, catching every drop of dayglow and refracting it into diamond sparkles.

Nicki pressed her forehead against the icy glass, remembering her six-year-old self doing much the same thing on a snowy morning in the Smoky Mountains, before everything went so awfully, irrevocably wrong.

Footsteps behind her drew her back to jaded reality, and she turned to see Dallas Cole enter the kitchen. He moved with a painful hitch that made her own back ache in sympathy, and the night's sleep had done little to return color to his cheeks or vigor to his demeanor.

"You look like you could use another week's sleep," she murmured, reaching for the empty cup she'd set out for him earlier. "Coffee?"

"Please." He groped for the back of the nearest chair and settled down at the small table in the window nook.

"Creamer? Sugar?"

"Just black." He looked at the frosty window. "How much snow did we get?"

"Just a couple of inches."

His dark eyes narrowed as she set a cup of steaming coffee in front of him and took the chair across from him. "Did you sleep okay on the sofa?"

There was a strange tone to his voice that she couldn't quite read. "Yeah, it was fine."

"Thanks for letting me have the bed. Very comfortable." He took a sip of coffee, grimacing. She'd made it strong.

"Sure you don't want some creamer?"

"It's perfect." His gaze flicked up to meet hers. "Did I miss anything while I was dead to the world?"

There was that odd tone again. "Just the snow."

"Right." He looked down at the coffee in his cup.

"Is something wrong?"

He shook his head, not looking at her. "No."

Now she knew something was wrong. But he clearly didn't intend to tell her what it was, so she let it go for the moment. "That bump on your jaw went down overnight."

He lifted his fingers to the abraded spot where his face had grazed the pavement when he fell, wincing at the touch. "Should've seen the other guy."

"What other guy, exactly?"

His gaze flicked up to hers again. "Other guy? You know I got this when I hit the pavement."

"You didn't get in that condition by yourself." She had a pretty good idea how he'd ended up wandering in the woods, but she couldn't exactly reveal what she knew to Dallas Cole or anyone else.

Her life depended on folks in River's End believing she was an ordinary fry cook with some medical skills that might come in handy for a group of people who didn't want the authorities looking too closely at their activities.

"Doesn't matter now." He took a long drink of coffee.

"You still don't want to call the police?"

"No." He set the coffee cup on the table. "I should probably get out of your hair, though. If you can just point me toward the nearest town."

"Southeast," she said, keeping her tone light. "If you were in any condition to walk across the room, much less three miles over the mountain."

"I'm tougher than I look."

She couldn't stop a smile. "Right."

"You could say that with a little more conviction." With a sigh, he rose from his seat and turned to look out the frosty window.

Nicki sucked in a gasp at the sight of a streak of blood staining the back of the borrowed jersey. "You're bleeding."

He turned his head to look at her. "Where?"

"Your back." She got up and started to tug up the hem of the jersey.

He turned quickly, putting his hands out to stop her. "It's nothing."

"Let me look."

He closed his hands around her wrists, his grip unexpectedly strong. Tension rose swiftly between them, electrified by Nicki's sudden, sharp awareness that beneath the facade of weakness, Dallas Cole was a large, imposing male with chiseled features and deep, intense eyes that made her insides liquefy with appalling speed.

Desire flickered in her core, and she tugged her wrists free of his grasp. She took a step back, swallowing the lump that had risen in her throat. "I'm pretty good with a first-aid kit."

He probed behind his back with one hand, his fingers returning bloodstained. He looked at the red wetness with dismay. "Damn it."

"I should treat that. Don't need you bleeding all over everything."

"No," he agreed, reaching for the back of the

chair as if his legs were ready to give out beneath him. "Can you do it here?"

"Of course. I'll be right back."

When she returned with the first-aid kit she kept in the hall closet, she found him shirtless. He'd turned his chair around and sat hunched over the curved back, his arms folded under his head. An alarming Technicolor map of scrapes and bruises crisscrossed his back, including an oozing arch of abraded skin just across his left kidney.

She kept her horror to herself as she unpacked the supplies she needed to treat the wounds. "This is going to hurt."

"What's new?" he muttered against his arms.

She pulled up a chair and sat beside him. "I'm going to clean everything first, then put antiseptic in any open areas."

"Are you going to do a play-by-play of your torture?" he muttered.

"Only if you keep up the surly attitude," she retorted, pressing a disinfecting cleansing pad to his back.

He sucked in a sharp breath at the sting.

"Sorry," she murmured, wincing in sympathy. There'd been a time when she had considered a career in medicine. Well, of sorts. She'd been a licensed first responder when she was living in Nashville a few years back. But she'd found herself ill-suited for the job. Other people's pain bothered her too much, making it hard to stay objective and focused.

Even now, acutely aware that the battered man sitting before her might be a very bad man indeed, she couldn't help but feel twinges of empathetic pain as she cleaned the abrasions that marred the skin of his back.

"You seem to know what you're doing." He turned his head toward her, peering at her through one narrowed eye. "You a nurse?"

She shook her head. "Used to be an EMT, though."

"Used to be?"

"I gave it up for a career in the hospitality business." She smiled at his arched eyebrow. "I'm a fry cook at a place called Dugan's in town."

"I see."

"No you don't. Nobody ever does." She probed gently at his rib cage, feeling for any sign of a fracture.

He sucked in another sharp breath. "Couldn't stand the sight of blood?"

"Too many whiny patients," she said lightly. "Gave me headaches."

"And restaurant customers are a step up?"

"Fry cook, not waitress. I only deal with whiny servers." She blotted the oozing scrape over his kidney. "Any idea what made this wound?"

He didn't answer, and her imagination supplied a few answers she would have given anything not to visualize. But she'd already seen some of the brutality members of the Blue Ridge Infantry could mete out. Some of them enjoyed inflicting pain a little too much, as a matter of fact.

"You must've really pissed somebody off," she murmured as she covered the raw scrape with sterile pads and taped them into place.

His back arched in pain as she pressed another sterile pad into place. "I have a bad habit of doing that."

"What are you, a tax collector?" she joked.

Before he could respond, she heard the trill of the telephone coming down the hall. For a moment, she considered just letting it ring, but it might be the call she'd been waiting for.

"Wait right here," she said and headed to the bedroom.

It was Trevor Colley on the phone. He was the manager at Dugan's. "Can you work the morning shift?" he asked. "Bella's stuck over in Abingdon looking in on her mama because of the snow."

She paused, torn. Normally, she jumped at working as many hours at the diner as she could, both for the money and for the opportunity to rub elbows with the militia members and their wives and girlfriends who frequented the diner on a regular basis. She'd made friends with some of

the women already, and an incident a few weeks
ago had even earned her the respect of a couple
of the men.

"Del McClintock is here."

She straightened. "Yeah?"

"He asked if you were coming in." Trevor kept
his voice light, but she heard a hint of disapproval
in his voice. The militia men might be good-pay-
ing customers, but the manager had never seemed
particularly happy about their patronage. He took
their money, of course. He'd be a fool not to, given
that in this impoverished part of the county, paying customers could be hard to come by.

But he wasn't exactly happy about his best fry
cook befriending members of the Blue Ridge Infantry.

Nicki did her best to straddle the line between
her manager's feelings and her own need to make
inroads into the BRI's inner circle. It could be a
delicate dance at the best of times.

But even Trevor, as much as he disliked the
hard-eyed men who ate daily at the diner, wasn't
above using her interest in them to get his way.
"Should I tell him you're coming in?"

She pressed her lips together as she considered
her options. Del McClintock's sexual interest in
her presented a very tempting opportunity to get
a little closer to her target.

But what was she going to do with Dallas Cole

while she was working a shift at the diner? The last thing she wanted to do was leave him here on his own while she worked a few hours at the diner.

No telling what kind of trouble he could get into.

THE MURMUR OF Nicki's voice drifting down the hall was like a lure dangling in front of a hungry bass. Dallas couldn't have resisted the temptation to hear what she was saying any more than he'd have turned down a juicy steak after three weeks of near starvation.

Urging his aching body into motion, he moved as quietly as he could down the hallway until he could hear Nicki's end of the conversation.

"And Davey can't come in?" There was a brief silence, then she sighed. "No, I get it. Everybody else has family to see after, except me. I'll be there in a few."

She must be talking to someone at the diner where she worked, he realized. He eased away from the door and turned to go back to the kitchen. But his foot caught in the carpet runner in the hall, tripping him up. He landed against the wall with a thud, the impact eliciting a grunt.

Before he could tamp down the pain in his bruised ribs enough to breathe again, Nicki emerged from the bedroom, her blue eyes flashing.

"What the hell are you doing?" she challenged. "Eavesdropping?"

His pain-fogged brain tried sluggishly to catch up. "Bathroom."

Her dark eyebrows arched. "You passed it to get here."

Damn.

"What did you expect to overhear?" she asked.

Ah, hell. Maybe he should just tell her the truth. "How about why you left the cabin for an hour last night in the middle of a snowstorm?"

Her eyes narrowing, she took a step away from him until her back flattened against the wall. "What are you talking about?"

"You left the cabin shortly before midnight and disappeared into the woods for over an hour. Then you snuck back in here, real quiet, and settled down for the night. Want to tell me where you went?"

"You were asleep at midnight. I checked on you."

"You thought I was asleep. I wasn't."

A scowl creased her forehead. "You were spying on me?"

"You woke me when you started to leave. I got curious. You're not the only one who spent the night with a stranger, you know."

"You're still alive, so I guess I'm not a serial killer." She folded her arms across her chest, angling her chin at him. In her defiance, she seemed to glow like a jewel, all glittering blue eyes and ruby-stained cheeks.

A flush of desire spread heat through his body, making his knees tremble. He flattened his back against the opposite wall of the hallway and struggled to stay upright beneath the electric intensity of her gaze.

She was dangerous to him, he realized.

In all sorts of unexpected ways.

He pushed himself upright, willing his legs to hold his weight. "You know, I think I should call someone."

Her suspicious gaze was as sharp as a blow. "Who're you going to call?"

"You've got a sheriff's department around here, right?"

Her scowl deepened. "They're probably a little busy today. With the snow and all."

"Not like it was a blizzard." His legs were starting to ache, from his hips to his toes. He fought the urge to slide down the wall to the floor.

"No, but in this part of the state, people aren't used to driving in snow."

"But you're going to, right?"

"What do you mean?"

"You're going in to work aren't you?" He nodded toward her bedroom. "That's who you were talking to on the phone."

"So you *were* eavesdropping."

No point in denying it. "You can drive me into town with you. I'll take it from there."

Alarm darkened her eyes. "No. I can't do that."

The first flicker of fear sparked through him. "Why not?"

"You don't want to go into River's End."

He urged his legs into motion, edging back from her. He hadn't seen any sort of weapon in his limited exploration of the cabin, but he hadn't exactly looked in every nook and cranny while she was gone last night. In fact, there were parts of the cabin that were still a complete mystery to him. She had already told him she had a shotgun. For all he knew, she could have a whole armory stashed somewhere in the back.

"Why don't I want to go into River's End?"

She moved with him as he stepped backward, maintaining the distance between them without letting him get out of reach. "Don't be coy, Dallas."

There it was again. He'd heard that same tone in her voice the night before, when she'd spoken his name while trying to help him into her Jeep. A flicker of knowing that hadn't really registered in the midst of his stress the previous evening came through loud and clear this morning.

"You know who I am," he said before he could stop himself.

Her expression shuttered. "Who you are?"

"Now who's being coy?" A surge of anger eclipsed his earlier fear. She was lying to his face. Had been lying this whole time. "If you know who I am, then you know there are people who are looking for me."

She dropped any pretense. "That's abundantly clear from the bruises and scrapes all over your body. Which is why I don't think you really want to go into River's End this morning."

His legs began to tremble again, aching with fatigue. "They're in town, aren't they?"

She didn't ask who he was talking about. Clearly, she already knew. "Yes. And not just in town. They're all over the place, Dallas. Everywhere you could possibly go."

Damn it. Fear returned in cold, sickening waves, but he fought not to let it show. Those bastards who took him captive had worked damn hard to break him, but they hadn't. He'd escaped before they could.

He wouldn't break in front of this woman, either.

"Then let me call someone to come get me."

The look she gave him was almost pitying. "I can't let you do that, either."

He forced a laugh, pretending a bravado he didn't feel. "And you're going to stop me how?"

Her response was a laugh in return. "You say

that as if you think it would be difficult. I told you last night, in your condition, I'm pretty sure I can take you."

He didn't really want to test her theory, considering how shaky his limbs felt at the moment. "Okay, fine. I'll stay put."

Her eyes narrowed a notch. "I don't think you will."

Before he could move, she closed the space between them, grabbing both arms and shoving him face-first into the wall. Pain exploded where his bruised jaw hit the hard Sheetrock.

He struggled against her hold, but she was much stronger than he was at the moment, shoving him down the hall and into the kitchen. When he tried to turn around to fight back, she slammed her knee into the back of one of his, making his leg buckle under him. She released his arms just long enough to let him catch himself before he lunged face-first into the floor, but he still hit hard enough to drive the breath from his lungs.

The world went black around him for a moment, then started to return in flecks of light as he gasped for air. He felt movement, pressure and then a big gulp of sweet air filled his lungs. His vision cleared and all his aches and pains came into sharp, agonizing focus.

He was facedown on the floor, his hands

twisted behind his back. He felt the weight of his captor settle over the backs of his thighs as she held him in place. The unmistakable sound of duct tape being ripped from its roll reached his ears a split second before he felt her wind the sticky tape around his wrists, binding his hands together behind him.

Nicki moved off his legs and grabbed him by his upper arms, her grip like steel. She might be small, he thought, but she was a lot stronger than she looked. "Sorry to do this, but you leave me no choice."

The fear returned, beating at the back of his throat like a wave of nausea. He swallowed it down, refused to give in. "And here you promised you weren't a serial killer."

"Believe it or not, this is all about keeping you alive." She got him to his feet and pushed him toward a door he hadn't noticed before. "Watch your step."

She opened the door and reached inside, flicking a switch. He saw he was standing at the top of a steep set of stairs descending into a dim basement. "You're not going to chain me to your dungeon wall, are you?" He tried to keep his voice light, make it into a joke. Anything to keep the fear at bay.

She helped him down the steps, grabbing the wood railing on one side of the descent when he stumbled and nearly pulled her down the stairs with him. "Sadly, I haven't had time to put in the shackles yet."

They reached the bottom of the steps and she gave him a little shove. He stumbled forward into the shadows, wincing in anticipation of the impact.

His upper body hit something soft. Opening his eyes, he saw he'd landed face-first on an old, overstuffed sofa braced against the cinder block wall of the basement.

Cellar, he amended mentally, his eyes beginning to adjust to the low light. There was a shelf against the opposite wall full of Mason jars full of home-canned fruits and vegetables.

"Stay put. I'll be back in a couple of hours." Nicki's voice drifted down toward him from the top of the stairs. He looked up at her, squinting at the bright daylight backlighting her through the cellar door, rendering her little more than a curvy silhouette.

"Don't go," he called, fear hammering past his last defenses.

She paused in the doorway. When she spoke, she sounded genuinely distressed. "I'm so sorry. But I have to go."

Then the door closed behind her, shutting out the blessed daylight. He heard the soft thuds of her footfalls drift into a thick, deafening silence.

Once again, he was alone. Trapped and helpless, just like before, with nothing but darkness and fear to keep him company.

Chapter Four

What have I done?

The question rang in her head, over and over in rhythm with her pounding heart, as she muscled the Jeep down the mountain to the main road that led into town.

She'd tied a man up and locked him in her cellar. Had she lost her bloody mind?

The cell phone peeking out of her purse presented a powerful temptation. She had never felt this great a need to talk to another human being in her life. Calling Alexander Quinn was out of the question—he'd never answer a call from her cell phone and risk blowing her cover.

But her cousin Anson might answer. She could shoot the breeze with him, avoid anything incriminating. Just hearing a friendly, familiar voice might be enough to knock the edge off her nerves, right?

She dragged her gaze back to the road as her wheels slipped a little on the slick surface. No.

No calling anyone from her past, no matter how freaked-out she felt at the moment.

She'd agreed to this job. She knew what was at stake.

Hell, that was why she'd just imprisoned a man in her cellar, wasn't it?

Despite the weather, the parking lot of Dugan's Diner was half-full when she pulled her Jeep into one of the employee parking spots and entered the kitchen through the employees' side door.

The only other person in the kitchen was Tollie Barber, one of the kitchen assistants who helped out with food prep and handled some of the easier cooking duties. She was busy at the counter, processing potatoes for hash browns, her frizzy blond curls tamed by a hairnet. She darted a quick gaze at Nicki. "So much for a snow day, huh?"

Nicki tucked her own dark hair under a protective cap and headed to the sink to wash her trembling hands. She kept her tone calm and light, hoping her agitation didn't show. "Gotta snow a lot more than this to keep people away from breakfast at Dugan's."

Trevor Colley entered the kitchen from the front area, moving at a quick pace for a man his size. His barrel chest and linebacker shoulders seemed to take up half the kitchen when he stopped next to where Nicki was preparing the griddle. "You're a good 'un to come in so fast,

Nicki," he said in a gruff voice that rumbled like thunder. It was all the thanks he'd give her. Trevor wasn't one to gush.

"Quite a crowd for a snow day," she commented, cracking a couple of eggs for the first order clipped to the order wheel. Two eggs, sunny-side up, hash browns and bacon. "Something up?"

Trevor gave her an odd look. "You tell me. Del McClintock brought four of his boys with him. They brought their girls, too. Should I worry?"

Nicki supposed it was a good thing that Trevor believed she might know the answer to his question. It suggested that people were starting to connect her with the Blue Ridge Infantry. Which meant, hopefully, that the BRI members themselves were starting to think of her as one of them.

That was her goal, wasn't it?

"No, don't worry. If you have any trouble with them, come get me."

Trevor frowned at her but went back out to the front of the diner, leaving her and Tollie to get the orders filled.

As she laid out the strips of bacon on the griddle to fry, the image of Dallas Cole's rainbow-hued collection of scrapes and bruises filled her head. Her whole body went cold and numb, and for a second, she thought she was going to be sick.

Oh, God. She'd taped a sick, injured man's

hands behind his back and locked him in her cellar without even feeding him breakfast first. She hadn't even left him a bucket if he needed to go to the bathroom. Which he couldn't do with his hands duct-taped, anyway.

What the hell had she been thinking? Had she lost her ever-lovin' mind?

But what else could she have done? Dallas had insisted on calling the FBI. Maybe it had been a trick—maybe the whole thing was a setup to prove she wasn't who she said she was. Maybe it had been a test. But if that was the case, she had no idea whether she'd passed or failed.

But what if he was legit? She certainly couldn't let him bring the FBI swarming into River's End at this point. Even if it didn't end up blowing her cover, every BRI member in town would crawl back in the holes where they'd come from, and it'd be months, even years, before she could get this close to the group's inner circle.

She was doing what she had to do. She was. She just had to get through this morning and she could hurry back home and let him out before anything bad happened.

Assuming something bad hadn't already happened.

THERE WASN'T AN inch of his body that didn't hurt in some way, including the new scrape on his inner wrist from the nail protruding from the wooden shelf where the beautiful but treacherous Nicki kept her canned goods. But Dallas was damned if he was going to be bound and locked in by the time she got back from her shift at the diner.

Who the hell was she? Was she connected to the militia members who'd taken him captive a few weeks earlier? If so, why had it taken her all night to decide he was safer behind a lock and key?

Everything had changed when he told her he wanted to call the authorities. That had been the catalyst. He'd seen fear in her eyes, not unlike his own reaction when she'd pinned him down and taped up his hands. His mention of the authorities had made her feel just as trapped as he felt now.

But why? What was she hiding?

The tape around his wrists snapped apart as the sharp edge of the nail head finally broke through the last of the fibers. He pulled his arms apart, groaning as the stretched muscles of his chest and shoulders put up a painful protest. He worked them slowly for a moment, taking care not to make his condition any worse than it already was.

He had to find the strength to get past that locked door and get the hell out of this crazy woman's cabin.

There were no windows in the cellar, no doors

visible besides the one at the top of the stairs. As much as his wobbly legs protested the idea, he had to go upstairs and try to figure a way to get through the locked cellar door. Ramming it open was no option, given his weakened state.

But maybe he could pick the lock.

He'd already spent nearly an hour searching the cellar for something to cut himself free of the duct-tape bonds. He'd found a small, rickety cabinet in the corner that held a box of tools. He'd had no luck using the garden shears he'd found inside to cut himself free because he couldn't get the blades turned to the right angle behind his back to cut the tape. But there had been other tools in the box that might work to unlock the door, hadn't there?

He crossed to the box lying on the top of the rough-hewn cabinet and started to pick through the contents, looking for something—

There. A jumble of old paper clips, some of them hooked together, some twisted apart. If he was very lucky, the lock on the door at the top of the stairs would be a simple spring-driven lock, and he could use the paper clip to push it open.

But if it wasn't…

He grabbed a pair of pliers and twisted one of the bigger paper clips until he'd fashioned a crude tension wrench, then curled the tip of one of the smaller clips into a modified hook, hoping they'd work well enough to get the job done.

"Picking a lock isn't as hard as you'd think," an FBI special agent had told Dallas once, and then he'd proceeded to explain just how to beat a pin-and-tumbler lock. "It's all about the pins. That's how a key works—getting the pins in the right position to turn the cylinder."

He carried his tools up the steps and slid his makeshift tension wrench into the keyhole, turning it one way, then the other, until he was satisfied which way the cylinder had to turn to open. Applying a little pressure to move the cylinder just out of position, he inserted the second paper clip into the keyhole.

His hands shook and his legs began to ache, feeling as if they'd suddenly lost the ability to hold him upright, but he kept at his probing examination of the lock's internal workings. One by one, he painstakingly pushed the pins up until they caught on the ledge, clearing the cylinder. Finally, the last pin clicked into place, and he used the larger paper clip to turn the lock.

The dead bolt slid back into the door with a soft click, and he gave the door a push open.

He eased into the kitchen and looked around, squinting as bright daylight assaulted his eyes. Around him, the cabin was quiet and still.

He looked around the house to make sure he

was still alone, then checked out the front door to assure himself Nicki and the Jeep were still gone. Then he went into the bedroom to find the phone.

But it was gone, no longer sitting on the bedside table where it had been the night before.

He checked the floor on either side of the table and even crouched to check under the bed. No phone.

A room-to-room search of the cabin revealed no sign of the missing phone. Nor did he find a computer or any sort of modem or router with which to access the internet if he wanted to reach the authorities that way instead.

He sank into one of the kitchen chairs and willed his wobbly legs to stop shaking. He clearly wasn't going to be able to call in the cavalry, so he was going to have to get the hell out of this cabin on his own somehow.

But first, he needed something to eat. Some of his unsteadiness might be from sheer hunger. He pushed himself to his feet and crossed to the refrigerator, bracing himself to find it as empty as the bedside table had been. But the refrigerator was well stocked, and he grabbed a couple of eggs from the carton for his breakfast.

She had plenty of cookware in her cabinets, too. Made sense, he supposed—she'd said she worked as a diner cook, hadn't she? As he heated a pat of butter in one of the pans on the stove, he grabbed a couple of slices of bread from the bread box and stuck them in the toaster.

The smell of toasting bread and frying eggs made him almost light-headed with hunger, but once he'd wolfed down his breakfast, he felt considerably better.

But did he feel well enough to walk out of these woods to seek help?

He left the pans for Nicki to wash—the least she could do, considering she'd locked him in her cellar—and took another look around the house, this time for some sign of who Nicki really was and what had compelled her to lock him up rather than let him call the authorities for help.

She'd admitted to knowing who he was. Which meant she had to know that he'd disappeared somewhere between Washington, DC, and wherever he was now. That foul play was suspected.

Or was it? Did people think he'd disappeared on his own? He'd been on the phone with a man named Cade Landry when those BRI thugs had run him off the road and dragged him out of his banged-up car. But Landry had been a fugitive. For all Dallas knew, he still was. He might not have had the opportunity to tell anyone what he'd heard over the phone.

So what, exactly, did Nicki think she knew about him?

There were no personal items anywhere around

the cabin, he realized after another search of the place. She probably had her driver's license and other ID with her, since she'd taken the Jeep into town, but most people had other personal records scattered around the house, didn't they?

Back at his apartment in Georgetown, he had a whole four-drawer filing cabinet full of tax information, personal records, vehicle papers and more. He even had a box in his closet filled with things he'd kept from his high school and college days.

As far as he could tell from his search, Nicki had nothing like that stashed anywhere around the cabin.

He sat on the bed and looked around the small bedroom. Simple gray curtains on the window. Plain pine dresser that matched the bedside table. The bed was little more than a mattress and box set on a metal frame. No headboard or footboard. Plain gray sheets and pillowcases, plus a couple of matching waffle-weave blankets that acted as the bedspread.

A large woven rag rug stretched over the hardwood floor next to the bed, the hodgepodge of blues, grays, black and white offering only a little more color than the rest of the decor.

Drab surroundings for a woman as vibrantly beautiful as his hostess-turned-captor.

He pushed himself up from the bed and looked

around, trying to make sense of all that had happened to him over the past twelve hours. And no matter which way he looked, it all came back to the same thing.

Nicki.

Who the hell was she? And what did she want from him?

BY NINE THIRTY, the breakfast crowd began to thin out, but Del McClintock and part of his posse lingered, nursing cups of coffee and chatting quietly in one corner of the diner. Nicki wasn't sure he was actually waiting for her to end her shift, but Trevor kept shooting troubled looks between her and the corner whenever he popped into the kitchen to check on things.

Nicki ignored her boss, taking advantage of the lull in customers to clean the griddle in preparation for the next crowd of hungry diners. She also tried hard not to think about the man locked in her cellar, without much luck.

People didn't starve to death in two hours. And if worse came to worst on the bathroom end of things, she could run to the thrift store in Abingdon to pick up some clean clothes for him.

Everything would work out. She'd figure it out somehow.

Trevor stuck his head in the kitchen door. "Bella's here. Her mama's neighbor's takin' good care of her, looks like, so she told Bella to come on in for the lunch and dinner crowds. That is, if you're ready to leave." Trevor shot another look toward the dining room, where Del and his friends were still lingering at a couple of the tables near the window.

"Yeah, I'm ready. I know Bella wanted the hours, and I have some things to do today." Like release a man from her locked cellar and some-how figure out a way to convince him she wasn't some sort of psychopath.

But what about Del McClintock? The whole point of agreeing to come in for the morning shift was Trevor's comment about Del and some of the other guys from the BRI being there.

And now she was going to slip out the back and not even talk to him?

Damn you, Alexander Quinn.

One minute. She could take one minute to go say hi to Del.

She grabbed her purse and her coat, and headed out through the door leading to the front of the diner, ignoring Trevor's troubled look. Several of the people with Del had left while she was clean-ing up, but he was still there, along with Ray Bat-tle and Ray's girlfriend, Tonya. Ray sent Del a smirking look as Nicki approached.

"Hey there, Del." She pasted on a friendly smile. "Can't get enough of my cooking?"

"Never." Del smiled back at her, his straight white teeth flashing. He was a good-looking man, tall and hard-muscled, which couldn't be said of all the BRI members she'd met over the past couple of months. He was also better educated than most, which made her wonder why he'd hooked up with a group like the Blue Ridge Infantry.

Then again, there were lots of people in the world blessed with good genes and good fortune who didn't have the moral fiber to make anything of themselves despite the raw material.

Del had been in the army, or so he claimed. Nicki had no reason to doubt him. But he had left the service as soon as he could manage, coming back home to join his father at Cortland Lumber in a town a few miles east of River's End, working in the sawmill.

As in, the business owned by Wayne Cortland, one of the most ruthless—and efficient—criminals to operate in southern Virginia until his death almost three years earlier.

According to the files Alexander Quinn had given Nicki to study, Wayne Cortland had pulled together a disparate group of black hat hackers, mountain meth cookers and members of the Blue Ridge Infantry to fill his organization. The hackers were the brains, the BRI served as the muscle and the meth cookers were the source of money.

But ever since Cortland's murder at the hands

of his own son, those three groups had been struggling to take over the remains of the organization and keep it going on their own.

Nicki was pretty sure Del McClintock was part of the BRI's attempt to take over the drug business for themselves. And at least two or three of the guys in his entourage were hackers.

But what she hadn't yet discovered was who had taken over as head of the Virginia branch of the BRI. Quinn believed that the unknown leader might be the key to toppling the whole organization, from the group in Virginia to the branch in Tennessee.

What they needed was someone inside, close to the top man, who could funnel information to Quinn and, through him, to the authorities.

Nicki planned to be that someone. And thanks to a little tidbit Del had let drop a week ago, she had an idea how to make it happen.

"Were you serious about what you said last week?" she asked, lowering her voice so that only the people at Del's table could hear. "About me picking up some work for you? You know, medical work?"

Del's eyes narrowed, and she was afraid she'd overplayed her hand. But his expression cleared. "If you think you're up to it. It's not exactly legal."

"It's just me doing a little first aid as needed, right?" She flashed him a grin. "And if you and your friends want to show me a little gratitude with gifts of cash, who's to say there's anything wrong with that?"

"Exactly." Del's smile was deceptively attractive, making him look genial and harmless when she knew he was anything but.

Nicki hid a little shiver and brightened her smile. "So you'll let me know if you need anything, right?"

"Absolutely." He winked at her. "Can you stick around?"

"I wish," she lied. "But last night I picked up a stray cat, and I'm afraid he's making a mess on my floors as we speak."

"We shoot strays at our place," Ray said with a grin.

You would, she thought. She forced a laugh. "I guess I have a soft heart. Or a soft head. Whichever. See y'all later." She gave a little wave and headed out the front door, keeping a smile on her face until she was certain she was safely out of sight.

She blew out a pent-up breath and allowed herself a little tremble. She had to figure out a way to get over her revulsion, especially if Del required her to be a little more than just friendly and flirtatious in order to give her the breaks she was looking for.

But the thought made her sick. Which was

silly, really—there'd been a time in her life when a guy like Del McClintock had been her particular brand of temptation. Dangerous, shady and handsome as sin.

Sort of like the injured man tied up in her cellar at home.

Damn it. What had she been thinking?

THE SOUND OF a vehicle engine drifted into the cabin, stirring Dallas from a light doze. He pushed himself up to a sitting position on the sofa, his nerves jangling, and tried to reorient himself as the engine noise grew closer. The nap on the sofa hadn't done much for his aches and pains, but he felt a little stronger than he had even this morning. Food and activity to work out the kinks from his weeks of captivity had gone a long way to restoring some of his earlier vigor.

But would it be enough to give him the edge over his feisty captor?

He glanced through the narrow gap between the curtains of the front window and spotted Nicki's Jeep pulling into the gravel driveway outside the cabin. She pulled to a stop and cut the engine, but she didn't get out right away.

What was she doing?

A minute ticked by. Then two. Dallas's legs began to ache again from the stillness of waiting.

When the Jeep door opened and she got out and

turned toward the cabin, he pulled back from the window and took up a position against the wall by the door. When she entered, the door would hide him until it was too late to prepare herself for his ambush.

At least, that's what he hoped.

Her footsteps ascended the wooden steps of the porch slowly. Deliberately. Inside Dallas's chest, his heart took a couple of hard leaps into a higher gear. He braced himself with a deep breath, preparing his limbs for action. He was still weaker than he liked, but his size and the factor of surprise would give him an edge.

He heard the rattle of keys in the door and pressed himself flat against the wall.

The door swung open with a creak of the hinges, and her boots hit the landing with a thud. He heard a soft huff of air escape her lungs as she stepped into the cabin and started to close the door behind her.

He hit her hard and fast, shoving her to the floor beneath him. Her soft cry of shock gave him the briefest moment of triumph, before his body landed flush against hers, his hips driving hers into the hard floor.

She started to struggle, her thighs opening as she kicked her legs toward him. The movement settled his hips more firmly into the cradle between her thighs, and, for a moment, he couldn't think. Couldn't come up with a single rational thought. All he could do was feel. The heat of her body under his. The softness of her curves, how perfectly they seemed to mold to his own lean hardness, welcoming him as if their bodies had been fashioned by a master craftsman to fit together in seamless perfection.

His heart rate soared, blood rushing south to where her sex cradled his. He exhaled, then sucked in another harsh breath as she stopped fighting and gazed up at him, her blue eyes dark and wide.

His hands tightened around her wrists, holding her captive on the floor beneath him, and she still didn't move.

When she spoke, her voice was a husky growl. "Did you get anything to eat?"

Chapter Five

There was a roar in her ears, like a winter wind rushing through the pine boughs. Her blood pulsing in her ears, she realized, hard and fast. Maybe that's why she thought she'd heard herself ask if he'd gotten anything to eat.

Because surely she hadn't just blurted such a thing to the wild-eyed man who held her pinned beneath him on the cabin floor.

The grip of his hands on her wrists loosened. His hips shifted, pulled away from her body, as cold air rushed in to replace his heat. He rolled onto his back beside her, gazing up at the cabin ceiling.

"Who *are* you?" he asked the ceiling.

She looked up to see what had drawn his gaze, but all she saw was slightly dingy white Sheetrock. "Are you asking me or the cabin?"

He rolled his head until his gaze met hers. "I made myself some scrambled eggs and toast."

So she *had* asked if he'd gotten anything to eat.

"How'd you get free?"

He hesitated a moment, as if considering what he should tell her. Finally, he sighed. "There was a nail sticking out of the wooden shelves in the cellar. I used it to rip the duct tape."

He was still breathing hard, she realized. Taking her down had winded him a little, which meant that, while he was clearly stronger than he had been the night before, he wasn't exactly in fighting form.

She pushed herself to a sitting position, trying to ignore the inconvenient—and highly inappropriate—tingling in her girl parts. She really had the worst taste in men. "That explains how you got your hands free. But how did you get out of the cellar? That's a good lock."

"Even good locks can be picked,"

"By a graphic designer?"

He sat up and looked at her. "You really do know who I am, don't you?"

"Did you think I was bluffing?"

His eyes narrowed. "No. But what I haven't figured out yet is who you are. And why you thought locking me up was a better option than calling the cops. What are you hiding?"

She couldn't exactly answer that question, could she? She started to get up, bracing herself for any move on his part to stop her. But he merely sat on the floor, gazing up at her with curious brown eyes. "What am *I* hiding? You're the fugitive from the FBI."

He tucked his legs up and started to stand, grimacing at the effort. She stuck her hand out to help.

He stared at her outstretched hand. "Yes. I'm the fugitive from the FBI. Which makes me wonder why you balked at my offer to call the authorities to take me off your hands."

She bit her lip and withdrew her hand. "Right."

He pushed to a standing position, his jaw tightly set. "'Right' doesn't exactly answer my question."

"I have my reasons for not wanting the police or anyone else sniffing around here. Can't we just leave it at that?"

The look he gave her made his answer superfluous. "I really don't think so."

She sighed and lied. "I'm a moonshiner."

His sudden bark of laughter caught her off guard. "No, you're not."

"How do you know I don't have a still hidden somewhere around here?"

"Because I searched this whole bloody cabin while I was waiting for your return, and there's nothing remotely like a still in this place. Nor, by the way, is there a phone, even though there was one in my room last night."

"It's broken."

He shook his head. "No, it's not."

Damn it. When had she become such a bad liar? She used to be really good at spinning tales, stories nobody could ever poke holes in because she made them sound so plausible.

Smack-dab in the middle of an undercover operation was a very bad time to lose her touch in the deception department.

"Let's go back to my first question," he said. "Who are you?"

"Nicki."

"Nicki what?"

"Nicki North."

His brows descended a notch. "Nicki North. Okay. We'll go with that."

"Someone named Dallas really has no room to question another person's name." She crossed to the door and locked it. "You picked the cellar lock? Really?"

"I'm out, aren't I?"

"What did you use?"

A faint smile touched the corners of his mouth, hinting at an unexpected set of dimples in his lean cheeks. "Trade secret."

"I don't have a tension wrench down there, so you must have improvised." She tried to remember what sort of tools were in the cellar. There was a box down there that had been here when she rented the cabin, apparently left behind by the last tenant. It had been a jumble of odds and ends, screws, nails, a hex key or two, some rubber bands, and a few brads and paper clips. She hazarded a guess. "Paper clips?"

"Should have known you were the lock-picking type."

"I like to think I defy easy categorization."

He laughed softly. "I bet you do."

She didn't like the way he'd turned this conversation into an exploration of her secrets, so she pushed back. "Where have you been for the past few weeks?"

"Don't you know that, too?" he challenged softly, taking a couple of steps toward her. "You seem to know so much already."

Though he was still too thin and too pale to look fully dangerous, her spine stiffened at his advance. He'd been strong enough to take her down by surprise, and she wasn't completely sure she'd have been able to fight him off if he hadn't rolled off and let her go.

Unfortunately, that hint of danger was doing all sorts of mortifying, tingly things to her insides. And she'd been doing so well with her "stay clear of bad boys" resolution to this point, damn it.

"Why don't we start from the beginning?" she suggested, taking a step back to maintain the distance between them. "I read an article about your disappearance a couple of weeks ago. Apparently your boss at the FBI reported you missing."

"Really?" He seemed surprised to hear it. "Which boss?"

"Some Japanese name, I think."

"Michelle."

She didn't like the way he said her name, with a touch of affection. Was she just his boss or something more?

She gave herself a mental kick. *What the hell, Nicki?* "Right. Michelle isn't a Japanese name."

"Matsumara is." There was a touch of humor in his voice. "What else did the article say?"

"Probably a lot less than you could tell me," she answered. "Since it happened to you."

He looked at her, his brow furrowed, and she thought he was about to refuse to answer her question. But after a moment, his expression cleared and he turned away from her and walked toward the fireplace. He'd started a fire, she saw, wondering why she hadn't noticed it when she walked into the cabin earlier.

Maybe because her mind was preoccupied with how she was going to explain her reckless actions once she let him out of the cellar?

"It was a Friday," he began. "I left the office, packed a bag and started south toward Kentucky."

"You're from there, right?"

He frowned. "The article was that thorough?"

"The articles," she corrected lightly. "There was speculation you might have been heading there for the weekend, maybe to visit family or something."

His expression shuttered. "No family left there anymore."

"So you weren't headed to Kentucky?"

"I didn't say that. It's still sort of home, I guess."

"But you didn't make it there."

"No. I didn't." He picked up the fire poker and she tensed. But he merely prodded one of the logs, stirring up embers before returning the iron to its holder. "I realized I was being followed. And then, I was run off the road." He shrugged one shoulder. "Don't remember much about the accident, really. I think I might have hit my head."

"What *do* you remember?"

"Men. Six or seven of them. They were rough and didn't really care if they were hurting me. In fact, if my subsequent interactions with them are any indication, they probably enjoyed hurting me." He turned to look at her. "It doesn't matter. Yesterday morning, they left me alone and didn't lock the door. Maybe they thought I was too weak to do anything. I don't know."

"You got away?" She didn't mean to sound skeptical, but even to her own ears, her doubt was obvious.

"I got away." A touch of defensiveness darkened his voice. "I just started heading west. I knew I was somewhere on a mountain. I figured if I headed west, I'd reach civilization sooner or later."

"So you were walking through mountains all day?"

"Not all day. Sometimes I was hiding from the people looking for me."

Nicki tamped down a shudder. "You know they're probably still looking for you."

He nodded. "That's why I'm still here in this cabin instead of out there in the woods."

"The lesser of two evils?"

"Duct tape versus steel-toed boots in the ribs? Yeah, definitely the lesser of two evils."

She shook her head, feeling sick. "I'm sorry. I didn't know what else to do. If it makes you feel any better, I couldn't even concentrate at work for thinking about you in the cellar. I should have at least let you go to the bathroom before I locked you up."

He released a little huff of laughter. "And fed me, right?"

"You must think I'm a terrible person."

He shook his head, still smiling. "Where would I ever get that idea?"

This whole thing was just too much. Dealing with Del McClintock, who'd probably like to get in her pants, was bad enough. But dealing with this cipher of a man, whose pants were proving an unexpected temptation to *her*, had her feeling completely out of her element.

She'd worn a lot of hats in her short life, from go-go dancer at a Memphis club to an EMT in Nashville. Now she was a fry cook in little River's End, Virginia. What she wasn't, what she clearly had no talent for, was being an undercover operative for Alexander Quinn and The Gates.

She wondered if Agent X had left any word for her at the drop site. She hadn't even thought about stopping to check, so intent had she been on getting home to let her captive out of the dank cellar.

As a spy, she stank up the place.

"You can go. Whenever you want. Just do me a favor and wait until you're well clear of here to call your friends in the FBI, okay?" She waved toward the door. "You can take my Jeep. There's a train depot in River's End where you can even catch a train back to DC if you want. Leave the Jeep there. I can pick it up later with my spare key."

"How do you figure I'll be able to pay for my train ride out of here?"

Her heart sank. "I can probably come up with fifty in cash, but I don't know if that's enough for a ticket."

He nibbled at his lower lip, and she couldn't

seem to stop wondering what those teeth might feel like worrying the tender flesh of her earlobe.

Damn it, Nicki!

"You know, I think I might prefer to stick around." Dallas's tone was low and thoughtful. "I'm not exactly in fighting shape at the moment, so I'm not sure I'm ready to face an FBI interrogation in my current state." His gaze flicked up to meet hers, a dangerous gleam in those dark eyes. "And I do enjoy solving puzzles."

She didn't miss his meaning, but she feigned ignorance. "I don't have any puzzles around here. I'm not very good at them, myself."

He smiled, his dark eyes crinkling at the corners. "Don't play stupid with me, Nicki North. I may not know who you are or what you're up to, exactly, but I'm not blind. I know you're smart and resourceful. And maybe, if I stick around here long enough, I just might figure out what sort of game you're playing."

"I don't play games."

"Of course you do. We all do." He moved toward her, his pace steady but unhurried, giving her time to retreat.

But she couldn't make her legs move. It was all she could do to hold his suddenly feral gaze as he closed the distance between them.

"I'm good at games." His voice was a low

growl, barely more than a whisper. "And I play to win."

She lifted her chin, the challenge in his voice sparking through her like a jolt of electricity, firing up her own hidden resolve. "So do I."

If it was a game he wanted, it was a game he would get. Because he was right. Everybody played games.

But nobody played them quite as well as Nicolette Jamison.

His name was not Agent X, of course, but ever since Nicolette Jamison had referred to him by that moniker in one of her reports to Alexander Quinn, he'd found a certain humorous satisfaction in thinking of himself that way whenever he approached the drop site.

The name he was currently using was John Bartholomew, and he wasn't any sort of agent anymore. Hadn't been for nearly a decade, his nascent career with the CIA over almost before it began, thanks to his terrible timing during a black bloc protest in Athens not long after Greek police shot a teenager. He'd walked out of the hostel where he'd been staying and right into the path of a chunk of concrete that had caught him square in the temple.

At least, that's what he'd been told when he'd awakened nearly three weeks later in an Athens hospital with no memory of the previous two months of his life.

His notes on his surveillance operation were long gone by then. His hotel room had been thoroughly searched and sanitized within an hour of his injury, his station chief in Athens had told him with regret. His mission was compromised and the CIA didn't care that it hadn't been his fault. They had no further use for him.

After his recovery, he'd returned to the life he'd been planning before the agency had recruited him, working as a tax preparer in his father's accounting firm in Johnson City, Tennessee.

He'd hated every minute of it.

Thank God for Quinn. The old CIA hand had needed a man in southern Virginia, just across the border from Johnson City, for a mission his security agency had taken on.

Quinn had picked him.

The snow underfoot had turned slushy as the temperature rose above freezing shortly before noon. If the trees overhead weren't blocking the sunlight that had broken through the clouds after a gray morning, the snow would probably be gone altogether within an hour. But the canopy of shade would keep the crusty slush on the ground for a while longer, forcing him to walk carefully so he'd leave only a minimal trail of footprints in the snow.

He spotted the fallen log beside the drop site cave. The branch was sticking up, their signal.

She'd left him a message for Quinn.

He started toward the cave when the sound of voices carried through the cold air. Freezing in place, he scanned the woods for the source.

There. Two men in woodland camo topped the rise, barely giving him time to hunker down behind a clump of knotted vines. As long as he stayed still, he shouldn't be spotted.

He hoped.

The men were carrying .22 rimfire rifles propped on their shoulders. Dangling from their left hands were the limp carcasses of a couple of gray squirrels.

Hunters. Gray squirrel season in Virginia would be over at the end of the month, so these guys were probably trying to get in a few final hunts before March.

They passed the cave and the fallen log without so much as a glance, chatting quietly about where they should go after squirrels next. They walked perilously close to where he was hidden behind the twisted vines, but if they noticed him hunkering in hiding, neither of them gave any sign.

He waited until their voices drifted into silence before he moved, walking as rapidly as he dared to the cave to check the small stone cavity where Nicki Jamison left her missives for Quinn.

The message was there, as expected. He tucked the folded paper inside his shirt and melted back into the woods from where he'd come.

Only when he reached the privacy of his truck did he unfold the paper and read the message inside.

Eyebrows arching at the information, he started the truck and drove southeast.

Once he'd safely reached Abingdon, he pulled out his phone and dialed the number Quinn had given him. Quinn answered on the second ring. "Miller's Plumbing."

"Dallas Cole is alive. And guess who's nursing him back to health in a cabin in River's End, Virginia?"

Chapter Six

Nicki North was not her name. He didn't know what her name really was, but Nicki North sounded too much like an alias for Dallas to buy. But she really did seem to be a fry cook at a local diner, because he could still smell a delicious hint of hash browns and bacon lingering in her hair when she leaned close to check his wounds.

She touched his wrist just below the scratch he'd sustained while freeing himself from the duct-tape bindings. Her blue eyes rose to meet his. "This is new."

He nodded.

"You did it freeing yourself?"

"Yeah."

She dropped her gaze, looking troubled. "I'm sorry. I shouldn't have done that to you. I should have figured out something else."

"Taking men captive isn't your normal hobby?"

Her gaze flicked up. "No."

"That wasn't a serious question," he said, softening his tone.

"I wouldn't blame you if you thought I was a psychopath. Under the circumstances." She applied antiseptic to his new wound, wincing when he sucked in a sharp breath. "Sorry. Really, I'm sorry."

"You're afraid of something." He caught her hand as she started to pull away, holding her in place.

Her gaze met his and held. "I'm afraid for you. We both know you're in trouble. And River's End is full of people you do *not* want to run into."

"You've already delivered that message. Loud and clear. But what I can't figure out is why you still live in River's End if you're so afraid of the people around here."

"I'm not the one in danger." She said the words in an untroubled tone, but he didn't quite buy it. Beneath her calm, unhurried movements, he sensed a dark undercurrent of tension.

Maybe she was telling the truth. Maybe all her fear was for him.

But he didn't think so.

She finished bandaging his wrist and sat back. "That should keep you until I get back."

"You've got to go back to work?"

"No. I have to go check on a friend who's

home sick." Her gaze shifted away, a sure sign of deception.

"A friend?"

"A woman I know. Long story that I don't have time to tell." Her expression shuttering, she packed up the first-aid kit and stood, pushing her chair back from the sofa. "You should take advantage of the peace and quiet to catch up on your sleep."

"Good idea," he agreed.

She slanted a look at him as she set the first-aid kit on the mantel, but if she suspected he was insincere, she didn't probe. "I shouldn't be more than a couple of hours. I'll bring back some groceries and fix us a proper dinner."

"Don't go to any trouble."

That time she stopped in the middle of unlocking the door and turned to look at him. "You're being mighty accommodating."

"Where am I going to go?"

Her eyes narrowed a notch. "Where indeed?" She continued through the doorway and closed it behind her. He heard the rattle of her keys in the lock, shutting him safely inside.

He waited until he heard the Jeep's engine fade away before he began a slow circuit of the house, similar to the search he'd made before, after he'd freed himself from the cellar. But this time, instead of looking for incriminating evidence, he focused on trying to get a feel for the place in hopes of gaining a deeper understanding of the woman who lived there.

Like the simple bedroom, the rest of the cabin seemed sparsely furnished with anything that could be described as personal. Most of the furnishings were old and mismatched, but not in a particularly charming way. Instead, they seemed to be the products of a single day of shopping in a secondhand store, chosen more for utility than style.

Not at all what he expected from the woman who'd taken him down in her kitchen, taped his hands together and thrown him in her cellar.

He started a second turn around the cabin, this time looking in less obvious places. Drawers. Cubbyholes. Closets.

If the measure of the woman wasn't easily discerned from the surface of her life, then perhaps there were hidden places where all her deepest, darkest secrets lay.

After a second pass through the cabin without finding any obvious hiding places, he stopped in the middle of her bedroom and looked around, trying to figure out what hiding places there might be that were less than obvious. An alcove or a hidden trapdoor, something that he might not notice at a cursory glance.

The problem, he mused as he went from room

to room, was that he was out of his element. Despite the artistic nature of his public relations career in the FBI, his world revolved around computers. Being stuck in this little mountain cabin without a computer or cell phone in sight was proving to be enough technological deprivation to drive him crazy.

He'd always been good with technology, even as a boy in the backwoods of Kentucky where computers were a luxury. He'd made friends at school with David Price, whose father was a computer programmer at the college up at the university in Lexington. David had spent all his summers with his dad, picking up everything there was to know about how computers worked.

He'd taught Dallas everything he knew, which hadn't been a lot. David hadn't been that interested in computers, preferring sports and, later on, girls.

Dallas had liked sports and girls, too, but he'd found himself utterly fascinated by the language of code, how the tiniest changes—a symbol here, a number there—could entirely change how a system functioned.

Unfortunately, when it came time to go to college, he'd lacked the skills to get into school on a technology scholarship. Instead, he'd gone on an art scholarship and focused on finding a job that would get him out of the backwoods for good.

That had been graphic design, first with an ad agency in the Virginia town where he'd attended college, then a few years later, working for the FBI in their public information office.

It had been the FBI and their focus on providing their employees with new educational opportunities that had returned him to his first love. He'd struck up a friendship with some agents in the cybercrime division who had talked him into a training track that might put him in a position to make a career move.

He'd never considered himself special agent material, but computers were something he understood. He hadn't forgotten the things he'd learned as a boy, and college had allowed him to pick up new information and skills that he continued to expand and hone on his own time.

He was good with computers and even the cybercrime guys had let him in to their inner circle once they saw that what he lacked in training he made up for in raw talent and sheer desire.

But he wasn't an agent. And now, thanks to FBI Assistant Director Philip Crandall, he never would be.

He reached the small kitchen and looked around, losing hope. If she was hiding anything—and he knew she must be, given the way she'd reacted to his desire to call the cops—she'd hidden it well. If it was some secret she'd ferreted away on her computer hard drive, he could have found it without a lot of effort. Computers, he understood.

Low-tech backwoods women, however, were clearly a mystery he didn't have a hope of deciphering. Never had.

Meanwhile, his back was aching, his legs felt like rubber and the start of a five-alarm headache was pounding a path through his skull. Eschewing the chairs at the breakfast nook table nearby, he slumped to the floor where he stood, leaning back against the oven. As he started to let his eyelids drift shut, something in the narrow space between the refrigerator and the cabinet caught his cyc.

Pushing himself to his hands and knees, he crawled across the kitchen floor and took a closer look. The space was dark, but there was just enough light slanting into the tiny aperture to reveal something tucked inside the niche.

His hand would never fit into the space, but surely there was something—

He eyed the utensil rack over the gas range and spotted a long-handled barbecue fork. Groaning, he pushed to his feet and grabbed the fork, carrying it back to the refrigerator.

It took a couple of tries to snag his elusive target, but finally the fork caught the edge of whatever lay within the niche and pulled it toward him.

It was a large manila envelope with a string tie fastening it shut. There was nothing written on either side of the envelope, but he could feel a thick stack of something enclosed inside. Papers, maybe. Documents.

Secrets.

Carrying it to the kitchen nook table, he pulled up a chair and set the envelope in front of him. "Okay, Nicki North, let's find out what you're hiding."

He untwisted the string clasp and opened the envelope, dumping the contents on the table. There were notes, some handwritten, some typed. At least three dozen notes, all told.

He picked up the nearest one and started to read, almost breathless with anticipation. But as he took in the words contained in the notes, his anticipation slowly turned to deeper confusion.

What lay inside the envelope answered some of his questions, but they didn't solve the mystery of Nicki North.

They only deepened it.

KAYLIE PICKETT'S EYES were wide with fear when she opened the cabin door to Nicki and hurried her inside. "Keith's gonna be back in an hour. I ain't got long."

The hair on the back of Nicki's neck rose but she pushed down the fear. Getting caught here with Kaylie wasn't anywhere near the worst thing that could happen to her. She could talk her way out of it.

Kaylie was the one who'd suffer most.

Kaylie and the baby she was carrying.

"You sure I'm okay to take these?" Kaylie looked at the bottles of prenatal vitamins Nicki pulled from her purse and set on the kitchen table.

"You need to take these," Nicki said firmly. "And you can't be drinkin' any 'shine or doin' drugs—"

"I don't do that stuff," Kaylie said quickly, peering at the vitamin bottles with a furrow between her eyebrows. She looked up when Nicki didn't speak. "I swear."

"I believe you," Nicki said, wishing she was more certain.

"I used to do a little weed, but I don't do that no more."

"Well, be sure you don't do weed or meth or any of that junk. You want a healthy baby, don't you?"

"'Course I do."

"Just take one of these a day. And you want to eat well, too. Plenty of green vegetables, carrots, lean meats—"

"Are squirrels lean meat?" Kaylie asked with a sudden grin.

Nicki smiled back. "Depends on the squirrel."

Kaylie laughed and gave her an impulsive hug. "Thank you for this. Keith won't even think about gettin' me anything like this. He thinks it's all some government conspiracy to suck money outta his pocket."

He would, Nicki thought. Or, at least, he used that excuse to get out of doing things he didn't want to do. "I'd better get out of here before Keith gets home. You got somewhere to stash those where he can't find them?"

"I do." Kaylie walked her to the door. "Thanks again."

"No problem. You call if you need anything." As she started to open the door, she remembered she still hadn't hooked her home phone up again after disconnecting it when she left for work. It was still in the floorboard of the Jeep. She'd have to put it back in case Kaylie needed to reach her. "Try not to worry, okay? As long as you eat right, take those vitamins and try to avoid too much stress, you and the baby should be fine."

Kaylie gave a soft huff of bleak laughter. "No stress, huh? I'll work on that."

Nicki tightened her jacket against the cold wind rolling down the mountain, ruffling her dark hair and sending little needles of cold drizzle into her face. She didn't think it was supposed to snow again, but she hadn't really checked the weather since this morning, had she?

She turned on the radio, flipping stations until she found a news break. After a couple of minutes, the announcer got around to a quick weather report. Sleet in places overnight, but no more snow expected.

That was a relief, at least. She hoped to get back to the dead drop later that night to see if Agent X had picked up her message. It would be faster and easier to get there without dealing with snow.

Come on, Nicki. You know the possibility of snow isn't what's got your nerves on edge.

No, it wasn't.

She had to worry about what she'd find when she got back to the cabin. Was Dallas Cole still going to be there? Was the fear of his former captors enough to make him stay put until she could get word from Alexander Quinn?

The front door of her cabin was still locked when she inserted her key in the dead bolt. Letting herself in, she stopped in the doorway and scanned the empty living room.

She locked up behind her and started into the hall, tempted to call out. But caution stopped her. If she wasn't alone, there was a distinct likelihood that whoever else occupied the cabin might not be a friend. It was a possibility she'd had to live with every moment since taking the undercover job Quinn had offered her.

There was a light on in the kitchen. She took a bracing breath and entered the room.

Dallas sat in the kitchen nook, a cup of coffee cradled between his hands on the table in front of him. He looked up, his dark eyes serious.

A moment later, her gaze fell on the manila envelope sitting next to his elbow.

Blood rushed to her head, roaring in her ears. Her whole body went cold, then hot, then cold again, and for a moment, her knees felt as if they would buckle.

She fought the sudden weakness and forced herself to the table to take a seat in front of him, her gaze settling on the manila envelope. It was tied shut, the way she'd left it when she stuck it into the narrow space between the refrigerator and the cabinet.

She cleared her throat, feeling sick. "You've been busy."

He turned the cup around slowly between his hands. "Idle hands are the devil's workshop."

"Did you open it?" She looked up at him.

He gazed at her as if she'd said something terribly stupid. Which, she supposed, she had.

"Right." She nibbled her bottom lip. "Look, whatever you read, it's probably not what you think."

The left side of his mouth curved upward a notch, a dimple forming in his cheek. "It's not like it was encrypted."

She sighed. "What do you think you know?"

He pushed his coffee cup away and looked at her. "You're working with Alexander Quinn. Which means, you're probably working for The Gates. Right?"

She didn't answer him. She didn't see the point.

"That's why you know who I am, isn't it?" he prodded.

"It's not like your story didn't make the news."

"But you don't even have a television here."

She looked down at her hands.

He sighed. "There's no photo of me in that envelope."

"No."

"But you've seen a photo of me." It wasn't a question.

"There are newspapers in town." She knew that she wasn't giving away much outwardly. She might be a little rusty at lying, since she'd turned over a new leaf, but she was still pretty good at a poker face.

"Okay." He pushed the envelope toward her. "Most of what's in here are messages from

Quinn. At least, they're signed AQ. I'm assuming that's not short for al Qaeda."

She just looked at him, determined not to give anything away.

"These messages aren't encrypted. But they *are* cryptic. In case they fell into the wrong hands?"

She shrugged one shoulder. "This is your little theory. You tell me."

He shook his head. "Does Quinn think I've gone over to the dark side? Is that what Cade Landry told him?"

"Who?"

Dallas's lips flattened to a thin line. "Just tell me the truth, Nicki. Is that even your name?"

"Yes."

"Nicki North?"

She didn't answer.

"I don't believe that's your last name, but if you're undercover, I don't need to know. I just need to know what you're up to and whether or not I can help you."

"Help me?"

"Where did you go last night?"

She didn't answer.

"To pick up another message from Quinn? Or to leave one?"

He was too close to the truth. Everything she'd risked, everything she'd worked to set in place, could be destroyed with a single word to the wrong person. "I can get you out of here. Isn't that what you wanted?"

He looked at her a moment, a flicker of surprise in his dark eyes. "You're ready to let me go now?"

"I never wanted to keep you prisoner. I just—"

"You just didn't want anything to blow your cover." He reached across the table and put his hand over hers. His warm, callused fingers brushed across hers, sending an unexpected shiver up her spine. "I don't want that to happen, either. But I can help you."

"I don't know what you're talking about."

"Yes, you do. You're trying to get information on the Blue Ridge Infantry. Something about a guy high in the organization Quinn wants you to get closer to."

She tried not to flinch, but his words surprised her. Quinn's message about the unnamed leader of the BRI had been about as oblique as any message he'd ever sent.

So how had Dallas Cole figured out what Quinn was trying to say?

"That struck a nerve," he murmured.

She snapped her gaze up to clash with his and jerked her hand away from his. "What do you want?"

"Just what I said." There was an unexpected

vibrancy to his sudden smile, as if someone had just turned on the electricity inside him. "I can help you, Nicki. I want in."

Chapter Seven

"You want in?"

Progress, Dallas thought. She'd clammed up once she spotted the envelope on the table, and he'd begun to wonder if she'd remain mute forever more. But apparently his offer of help had surprised her enough to overcome her caution.

"Those people kept me locked up for three weeks. They were rough on me, trying to get information out of me that I didn't have. And I think they've managed to find allies in the FBI who will be more than happy to make sure I don't make it back to DC to tell my story. So I want in. I can help you."

"I never said I needed help."

"You haven't said anything at all," he pointed out. "The silent treatment is starting to bug me."

"You're crazy. You don't know a damn thing about me. You've read my personal letters from a friend and somehow come up with some wild tale about me being some kind of spy."

"Undercover operative," he corrected.

"Whatever."

He rose to his feet and stood over her, wondering if she'd intimidate easily. He had a feeling she wouldn't. "So, if AQ doesn't stand for Alexander Quinn, what does it stand for?"

"Alan Quincy," she answered without hesitation.

She was a pretty good liar, he had to admit. Quick and bold. And definitely not intimidated. "Boyfriend?"

"Old schoolmate."

"Really. What school?"

"Ridge County High School in Tennessee." She looked up at him, her expression placid. "He was a senior. I was a sophomore. We were both in the film club."

"Film club."

"We got credits for watching movies and writing about them. Total scam, but the school never called us on it." She flashed him a grin. "You should have read my essay on the symbolism in *Mean Girls*."

He couldn't stop a smile from crossing his lips in return. She was lying through her pretty white teeth—though he had a feeling she really had written one hell of an essay on *Mean Girls*—but he couldn't stay annoyed with her.

He was right, damn it. He knew she was working for Alexander Quinn. It was the only thing that made any sense of the past two days.

If she was really up to her elbows in the Blue Ridge Infantry, she'd have turned him over to the men he'd escaped. But she hadn't.

And clearly, she wasn't some normal person living in the woods, because she'd taped his hands together and left him locked in her cellar so he wouldn't leave while she was at work.

"Why did you lock me up?"

Her gaze, which had fallen to the manila folder he'd left on the table in front of her, lifted to meet his. "I told you why."

"To protect me."

She stared at him for a long moment. Then she put her face in her hands. "Damn it," she murmured, her voice muffled by her palms.

He eased himself into the chair across from her again, remaining silent while she muttered beneath her breath. Finally, she looked up at him, her eyes wide and scared. Fear radiated from her, infecting his own nerves until they hummed, deep and sonorous, with dread.

He'd told her he wanted in. And he'd meant it.

But the look in her eyes told him his declaration had been reckless.

"You're right, okay?" Her voice trembled. "You're right."

"Can you be more specific?"

She dropped her head in her hands. "I'm undercover. I'm trying to uncover the identity of the new leader of the Blue Ridge Infantry's Virginia branch."

"For Alexander Quinn."

She looked up. "For Quinn. For The Gates. For myself."

"For yourself?"

"Look, Quinn doesn't know this. And I don't want him to. Do you understand? I don't want him to know what I'm about to tell you."

The strangled tone of her voice sent alarm rattling down his bones. "I understand."

"Almost two years ago, I worked as a confidential informant for the Nashville Police Department."

He raised his eyebrows.

"It's a long story. I was in the wrong place at the right time." She shook her head. "Pretty much the story of my life. I had gone out a few times with a guy who, as it turned out, was one of the city's biggest fences. The cops all knew he had a shop somewhere but they hadn't been able to catch him at it. When they saw me with him, one of the cops approached me. He threatened to make sure I went down with Blake—that was the name of the guy, Blake Ridenour. But see, I really didn't know Blake was a criminal. I just thought he was cute and he treated me like a queen."

"Ouch."

"Well, when I found out who he really was, a lot of things started to make sense. Things I should have noticed before. I guess I just didn't let myself see the warning signs." She sighed. "Also the story of my life."

"Did you help the cops catch him?"

"Yeah. And he never knew it was me." There was a hint of pride in her voice. But that flicker of confidence faded quickly as she brushed her dark hair away from her face, revealing the graceful curve of her neck.

The urge to kiss a path down that long column of perfect skin hit him like a gut punch. He shoved the rush of desire deep inside him, clenching his hands together to keep from reaching out to touch her. "What does this have to do with the Blue Ridge Infantry?"

"After I proved myself with Blake, the Tennessee Bureau of Investigation approached me. They'd heard about me from the Nashville police and thought I was the perfect person for this particular job they had in mind."

"What kind of job?"

She met his gaze. "You're in the FBI. You know what a honey trap is, don't you?"

He nodded, feeling a little queasy.

"The TBI had been investigating reports of a

militia group, originally from Virginia, that had begun to spread into eastern Tennessee."

"The Blue Ridge Infantry."

"Yes." She pushed up from her chair and paced to the coffeemaker, pressing both hands on the counter and gazing at the half-full carafe. After a moment, she opened a cabinet and pulled out a mug. She remained quiet as she poured herself a cup of coffee and added cream and sugar.

Dallas stayed quiet, too, giving her time to gather her thoughts, though growing anxiety had begun to fray his patience. Whatever she'd been through seemed to have her thoroughly rattled, and he wasn't sure he wanted to know how bad a situation had to get to throw a woman like Nicki off her game.

She brought her cup of coffee to the table and sat again, cradling the warm mug between her palms. "It seemed an easy enough assignment. They hadn't had any luck getting anyone inside the militia, but there were people on the margins they thought could be exploited. One of those people was a farmer who lived in a tiny place called Thurlow Gap. He wasn't a member of the militia, but he had two brothers the TBI believed were members, and the farmer was known to be sympathetic to their cause."

"Your job was to get close to the farmer?"

She nodded. "He was recently widowed. His

wife had died of breast cancer the previous winter, and he was left to take care of three kids. He needed a live-in housekeeper and nanny, I guess you'd call it. The TBI had done a lot of research on the guy, down to the kind of woman his wife had been. And they coached me how to be as much like her as possible."

"Oh." He was beginning to get an idea just how this story was going to end. No wonder she looked sick.

"It wasn't supposed to get personal. Not really. I wasn't sent there to seduce him. It wasn't supposed to cross any lines that way."

"But it did?"

"Kind of." Her grip on the coffee mug tightened, though she still hadn't taken a drink. "He wasn't what I expected. He was nice. Decent. Still hurting from the loss of his wife. And those kids..."

He didn't miss the glitter of tears in her eyes. "What happened?"

"He wasn't as sympathetic to the militia as the TBI thought. He just loved his brothers. So he tried to protect them. And it ended up costing him everything."

"How?"

"I found out his brothers and their friends were planning an attack on some conservation officers who were doing license checks at a nearby reservoir. He'd been trying to talk them out of it, make them see the stupidity of doing something so destructive." She shook her head. "He sympathized with the idea of less governmental interference in the lives of its citizens. Hell, who doesn't? I know I do. But hurting or even killing people who are just doing their jobs—"

"You reported the plan to the TBI?"

"I did." She closed her eyes, tears squeezing through her eyelids and trickling down her cheeks. "But his brothers thought the information had come from him. So they made him pay."

"How?"

"They burned his fields. All his crops that would have paid the bills once it was time to harvest. But they didn't stop there." She dashed away the tears with quick, angry flicks of her fingertips. "Then they burned him out of his house. We almost didn't get the kids out in time."

"My God."

"He lost everything. His house. His living. Almost lost his children."

He reached across the table and took her hands. "You know it wasn't your fault."

"In my head I know it."

"You're not the one who set the fires. You're not the one who was planning murders."

"I told the TBI I was out. There wasn't anything more I could get for them, once that poor man's life was torn apart. And it wouldn't have done any good for them if I stuck around living a lie. So I said my goodbyes and I ran." She turned her hands palm up beneath his. "I ran home."

"Like I did."

She looked up at him. "Yeah. I guess exactly like that." Her grip on his hands tightened a notch. "Though I didn't get ambushed on the way."

"You sound as if you finally believe me."

"You didn't give yourself those scrapes and bruises." She dropped her gaze to their entwined hands. "There was always a question in Quinn's mind whether you were a good guy or a bad guy."

"You might want to ask a guy named Cade Landry his opinion." He tugged his hands, trying to pull them away from hers, but her grip tightened, holding him in place. "If he's even alive anymore."

"He's alive. And well."

Relief washed over him in a wave. He'd been almost certain Landry would be dead by now, thanks to his own stupidity. "Crandall didn't get to him?"

"Crandall?" She frowned at him. "Who's Crandall?"

She didn't know, he realized. But shortly before those thugs in trucks had ambushed him on the highway south, he'd talked to Cade Landry on the phone to warn him about Crandall.

Maybe Landry hadn't believed him.

"You're in contact with Quinn, right? You should ask him. Landry surely told Quinn what I told him about Philip Crandall."

"Maybe," she conceded, looking uneasy. "Quinn's pretty big on the whole concept of 'need to know.' But why don't you tell me what you told Landry? Because I think I need to know, and I don't think I can wait for Quinn to get around to agreeing with me."

"Philip Crandall is an assistant director at the FBI. And I'm pretty sure he's the one who sicced the BRI on me."

Nicki's eyes widened with alarm. "Assistant director at the FBI? The BRI has infiltrated the Bureau that high up?"

"I don't know," he admitted. "I just know that when I told AD Crandall what Cade Landry asked me to tell him, I got a very strong sense that I'd made a huge mistake."

"What did Landry ask you to tell him?"

"I think now it might have been a setup. Only problem is, I think I'm the one who got caught. And if I'm ever going to be able to get my life back, I have to prove that Crandall is dirty."

"How are you going to be able to do that?"

He met her worried gaze. "I have a few

thoughts. But first, I'm going to need a few things. And I think maybe you can help me out with that."

ALMOST ALL THE snow had melted off during the afternoon hours, but the dead leaves underfoot had remained damp enough to form ice crystals when the temperatures dropped after nightfall. They crunched far too audibly beneath Nicki's feet as she hiked up the mountain, making her nerves rattle.

There's nobody watching, she told herself, even as she scanned the woods for any sign someone might be following her. She was coming up from the town side of the mountain this time, on her way home from an evening shift at the diner, leaving her Jeep parked behind the hardware store in hopes she'd escape notice.

She'd left Dallas behind in the cabin earlier with a warning to let her handle this part of the plan alone, but he hadn't exactly followed any of her orders to date, had he? What if he'd changed his mind about striking out on his own?

He wasn't what she'd expected. Quinn had described him as a worker bee, one of the nameless, faceless drones who kept the bureaucracy functioning. A graphic designer working in the public information office, putting out flyers and brochures describing the wonders of working for the FBI or touting their most recent successes.

But the Dallas Cole who'd picked the cellar lock and hunted down all her secrets was anything but a drone.

And while she wasn't exactly a technophile, she knew enough about computers to realize that the list of supplies he was requesting from Quinn suggested a computer savviness she hadn't expected.

By the time she reached the dead drop, she was shivering beneath her layers of warm clothing, but she knew it wasn't a reaction to the cold. Her life had been complicated enough before Dallas Cole stumbled in front of her Jeep in the middle of a winter storm.

Now it was becoming downright dangerous.

Her signal was gone, replaced by Agent X's downturned log. She had a message from Quinn waiting for her already.

What was she going to do if Quinn wanted her to abandon the case? There was a part of her that was scared senseless now that she was so close to getting the information she'd come here to find. If she continued to play her cards right, Del would introduce her to the head of the militia group, the man who was looking for someone to be his personal medic. And Nicki could make her own case for being that medic.

They'd have his identity. They'd have her on the inside where she could see and hear things another woman wouldn't get close enough to see or hear. And in the Blue Ridge Infantry's world, women weren't good for much of anything but sex, housekeeping and the occasional object of a man's anger. She'd be little more than a piece of furniture, ignored or forgotten most of the time, a fact she intended to use against the bastards.

But so much could go wrong so easily. One misstep could cost her everything she'd been working for.

And Dallas Cole was a misstep waiting to happen.

Nicki found a small packet of papers stashed in the small alcove inside the cave. She normally waited until she got back to the cabin to read the messages Quinn left her, but this time, curiosity got the better of her and she pulled a small penlight from her pocket and scanned the notes.

The first two papers contained a concise but thorough outline of what The Gates knew about Dallas Cole. To Nicki's relief, Quinn's assessment seemed to track precisely with what Dallas had told her himself.

Before she could check the rest of the notes, she heard the murmur of voices somewhere outside the cave.

Nerves jangling, she extinguished the penlight and pressed herself flat against the cold stone wall of the cave, holding her breath to listen.

The voices were male, but she couldn't make out words. They seemed to be some distance away but moving closer. She might have time to leave the cave and get out of sight before they could spot her.

But what if she was wrong? If someone saw her sneaking around this cave, they'd become curious. If word got to the wrong person—

She edged toward the cave mouth but stayed inside, straining to hear the voices of the men headed her way.

Definitely two of them, she decided as they came close enough for her to make out their words. From their conversation she quickly discerned they were night-hunting for opossum. And one of the voices belonged to Del McClintock.

"I don't know why he wants possum, but I've learned not to ask questions." That was Del, his drawl spreading like warm molasses.

"He still doin' poorly?" the other man asked. Nicki tried to place the voice but couldn't. Might be one of the crew she hadn't met yet.

"Yeah, but we're working on that. Seems like what he needs most is someone to monitor him, make sure he's gettin' his meds like he's supposed to. You know he doesn't want to involve a doctor, so we're trying to work out a different deal."

"You mean that girl, don't you? The cook at the diner?"

Nicki held her breath.

"Yeah, turns out she has some paramedic experience or somethin', but I don't think that's really why he's interested." Del laughed. "Can't really blame him for wanting a nice piece of scenery like Nicki around. I wouldn't mind exploring a little of that scenery myself."

Nicki grimaced. She might be laying a honey trap with Del, but she didn't have to like it. On the upside, Del seemed to think the mysterious head of the Virginia BRI was interested in her services as a caregiver. He'd played pretty coy and noncommittal with her so far, so this was good news.

Wasn't it?

She waited for the two of them to move on, but their footsteps stopped just a few yards away from the cave. The urge to take a peek to see if she could spot Del and his companion was almost more than she could resist, but she plastered herself to the cave wall and tried to calm her rapid respirations.

"Is that a cave?" That was Del's voice, terrifyingly close. Nicki swallowed a moan.

"Don't look like much of one," the other man drawled.

Del's footsteps crackled the frozen leaves underfoot as he moved closer to the cave. "Might be a possum nesting in there. Why don't we go take a look?"

Nicki's heart skipped a beat.

Chapter Eight

She'd been gone awhile, hadn't she?

Dallas glanced at the clock on the wall over the fireplace. Only nine thirty. She'd wanted to wait until after her shift at the diner to check the drop site, preferring the cover of darkness to make her trip through the woods. She'd told him the hike up the mountain would probably delay her by about thirty minutes, so she'd be home around ten.

Which meant there was still half an hour to wait before he could panic.

He had to do something to get his mind off Nicki's trip into the woods. Surely there was something constructive he could be doing while he waited? He could certainly use more sleep, but he didn't think his nerves would let him settle down for a nap. He'd already walked three circuits of the cabin's small interior, trying to build up his stamina, but the repetition was about to drive him crazy, as well.

He could always study the notes from Quinn. He'd had time to glance through them before Nicki returned home, but she'd stashed them back in the space between the refrigerator and the counter soon after.

But she hadn't actually told him not to touch them again, had she?

No, he decided. A glare was not an actual warning.

He pulled the envelope from the niche and started to untie the envelope closure when he heard the front doorknob rattle. The door creaked open slowly, and Dallas held his breath, waiting for the all clear signal Nicki had promised before she left on her hike.

But it didn't come.

The footfalls on the hardwood floors of the front room sounded heavy and, well, male. The door closed with a soft click, there was a brief rattle of keys and Dallas heard a male voice quietly ask, "The lights are on. You sure she's not here?"

With his pulse pounding like a whole drum line in his ears, Dallas gathered up the papers as quietly as he could and looked at the dead bolt lock on the back door.

Please be a quiet lock. He edged over to the door and gave the dead bolt knob a slow twist. It glided open with only the tiniest of clicks.

"She's still at the diner, best I know. She never

gets out of there early. You know how Trevor works those girls. We'll have to work fast, but we should have time."

Dallas waited, listening. Listening to the little voice in his head as his grandmother used to call it. "Trust that little voice. It knows what's what."

In the front room, a scraping noise gave him the opening he needed. He turned the knob and opened the door, the slight creak hidden by the sound of chair legs sliding across the floor. He slipped through the narrow opening and pushed the door closed, turning and running for the woods behind the cabin.

He didn't stop until he was several yards deep in the woods, his lungs aching from the cold air. He hadn't had time to grab his jacket, and the borrowed sweats felt inadequate to combat the frigid temperatures for long.

He tugged the papers tightly to his chest and looked for anything he could use for shelter, but all he saw was trees, trees and more trees. He tamped down his dismay and just breathed, in and out, filling his aching lungs with clean mountain air until the rushing sound in his ears subsided.

Think, Dallas. You used to know the hills and woods like a friend.

He looked around again, this time without the rush of panic and despair. There were plenty of broken limbs on the ground, victims of past storms. Some of them were pine boughs—he could use them to construct a simple shelter to at least block out the wind.

He secured the papers back in the manila envelope and tucked them inside his sweatshirt for safekeeping while he went to work constructing his shelter.

Hunkering down in his cramped little pine bough fort a few minutes later, he finally had time to breathe and think about the intruders and what they might want. Nicki had told him she was trying to get on the inside of the BRI, so it made sense that they'd want to check her out a little more thoroughly. But entering her cabin to do a search when she was due home in under an hour suggested a brazenness that gave Dallas a very bad feeling about Nicki's infiltration plan.

What the hell was Alexander Quinn thinking, putting her into such a dangerous situation?

The cold was a living thing, with icy fingers that crept beneath his clothing and traced a shivery path down his spine. He tucked his knees up and curled into a ball, wishing he'd had time to grab a jacket. Not that it would have been much protection against the frigid night air. Nothing would protect him from the cold if he had to stay out here much longer.

He tried to calculate the time that had passed

since he'd checked the clock over Nicki's mantel. Ten minutes? Twenty? His watch had been one of the casualties of his abduction—his captors had stripped him of anything that could ground him in the world he'd left behind. He'd lost track of time, of day and night, even of who he was from time to time.

But he knew who he was now. He knew where he was. He knew it was night, it was cold and if Nicki came back to her cabin now, she'd walk in on an ambush.

He couldn't let that happen.

Pushing aside the pine boughs covering his makeshift fort, he rose to his feet and headed back toward Nicki's cabin. He wasn't sure what he was going to do when trouble came, but he'd do something even if it killed him.

He'd done all the cowering he planned to do for a lifetime.

"I DON'T THINK possums hide in caves." The voice of the unknown man carried into the cave.

Nicki flattened her back against the cave wall and tried to breathe quietly, despite the ache in her lungs. She couldn't risk drawing the attention of the men outside. There was nowhere to hide. Nowhere to run.

And if Del McClintock caught her in here and

saw what she'd been hiding all these weeks, she'd never get out of River's End alive.

"I wonder if Craig and Ray are done at the cabin yet." Del sounded curious but not worried.

What cabin? Nicki wondered.

"You sure she's not there?" the other man asked.

"Her shift ended at nine, and you know Trevor keeps his crew workin' for another hour or so, spit-shinin' everything for the next day. She ain't gonna be home for another hour. They got plenty of time to take a good look around."

Oh, no. No, no, no.

Two of Del's boys were at her cabin, doing a search?

Dallas was as good as dead.

"There's a place down the mountain a ways where I think I saw a possum nest last spring. Want to take a look there?" Del asked.

"Sounds good."

Nicki kept her feet until she could no longer hear their footsteps crunching through the leaves. Then she slid down to the cave floor and took deep gulps of breath while her heart rate slowly returned to something close to normal.

Oh, God. That was so close.

She didn't let herself fall apart for long. She had to get to her cabin and find out what the hell was going on.

She hurried down the mountain to retrieve the Jeep, wishing like hell she had put the phone back on her bedside table. She just hadn't quite trusted Dallas enough to leave him alone with a line to the world outside, and that lack of trust had just come back to bite her.

She tried not to speed on her way home, well aware that in a town as small as River's End, even a traffic ticket managed to find its way into the town's grapevine sooner or later. Someone might wonder why she'd been on that particular road when it wasn't the most direct route home to her cabin. Or why she'd been so frazzled when she was pulled over.

Easing her foot off the accelerator, she took her time, concentrating on the one good thing that had come from the conversation she'd overheard. The head of the Virginia BRI was seriously considering taking her on as his personal caretaker. That meant she would find out who he was and would be uniquely positioned to find out what kind of trouble they were planning these days.

Unless Ray and Craig found something incriminating at her cabin. Like Dallas or that envelope full of messages from Quinn.

Stupid, stupid, stupid! Why had she held on to those messages?

Because they made you feel less alone.

Not a good enough reason. Not nearly good enough, especially now.

The gravel park in front of her cabin was unoccupied when she arrived. That meant nothing, however, she realized as she pulled the Jeep into its usual parking space. Ray and Craig didn't live that far away. They could have easily come here on foot to do their search of her cabin.

She should have been expecting something like this, she realized. She was a terrible excuse for a spy.

The front door was locked when she turned the knob. Which meant they had a copy of her keys. The thought made her skin crawl, and she made a mental note to change the dead bolt the next chance she got. And then make sure her keys were never out of her possession.

She unlocked the door and entered cautiously, in case they were still inside. There was a light on in the front room and also in the kitchen. Her cabin was isolated enough that she hadn't thought it necessary to warn Dallas to keep the lights turned off. Who would be passing by?

Craig Lafferty and Ray Battle, as it turned out, she thought grimly, some of her fear eclipsed by a rush of blazing anger. How untouchable did they think they were, that they could just break into her cabin at will and go through her things?

They're criminals, Nicki. What do you expect?

She clicked a button on the small black remote on her key chain. Most people assumed it was a remote entry device for her Jeep. It wasn't. Instead, it was some contraption the security guys at The Gates had come up with to detect both trackers and listening devices. If there was a bug in her cabin, this little device would detect it.

Nothing. Whatever else Craig and Ray had done, they hadn't put a listening device in the cabin.

She pocketed her keys and made a slow exploration of the cabin, room to room, trying to hold back the acid panic eating a hole in her chest. She had to keep her head. Think clearly rather than react.

She had to give the boys credit—they had been careful not to leave a big footprint with their search, but she spotted subtle signs that someone had been inside the cabin. Her hairbrush wasn't on the same side of the bathroom sink where she normally put it. In the bedroom, the closet door was closed completely, where she left it open a crack during the winter so the heat from the bedroom could keep her clothes warm for those early morning drives to the diner.

And worst of all, there was no sign of Dallas anywhere in the house.

Had they found him here? Had they taken him captive once more, to inflict God only knew what kind of tortures on him? Or had they taken him into the woods out back and killed him?

Stop. Stop thinking the worst. Just keep looking.

She entered the kitchen and looked around. One of the chairs at the table was out of place, but there was no sign of a struggle here any more than there had been anywhere else in the house. That was a good sign, wasn't it? Dallas wasn't in top form, but he wouldn't have let those guys grab him without a fight.

So maybe they hadn't found Dallas after all. But had they found her messages from Quinn?

Holding her breath, she checked the niche between the refrigerator and the counter.

Her heart sank.

The envelope was gone.

That was that. Big break or no big break, she'd just worn out her welcome in River's End and it was time to pull up stakes and get her tail back to Tennessee while she still had time to get there alive.

She knew how to travel light, and this was clearly one of those moments where speed was more important than thoroughness. She grabbed a backpack from her closet and threw in a couple of changes of clothing and a few pairs of sturdy shoes. The strappy high-heeled sandals she'd bought in Abingdon last month would have to stay in the closet, along with the dress she'd splurged on because it went so well with the shoes.

There was a first-aid kit in the back of the Jeep, and a Leatherman tool in the glove compartment. There was a Swiss army knife in her purse. She grabbed a few snack bars from the cabinet and a six-pack of bottled water from the refrigerator.

That should be enough to get her safely to Purgatory, Tennessee, by sunup.

The sound of the back door opening made her nerves jerk, and she whirled around, ready to swing the six-pack of water like a bludgeon.

Dallas Cole stood in the doorway, looking haggard and pale. He was shivering but a slow smile spread across his face, digging dimples into his lean cheeks. "You look like you've seen a ghost."

"Are you all right?" The urge to throw herself in his arms almost overcame her good sense.

"I'm freezing to death and I just spent an hour trying to figure out how to take on two big mountain men with just my sparkling wit and winning personality. But other than that, I'm just dandy." He closed the distance between them, raising his hands to her face. His fingers were icy and she gave a little start, but when he started to pull his hands away, she put the water bottles down on the table beside her and put her own hands over his, holding them in place.

"You got out in time?"

"I did." His brow furrowed. "You already knew, didn't you?"

"That someone came in here while I was gone? Yeah." Was it her imagination or was his face suddenly a lot closer?

"Because I was missing?" His breath warmed her lips.

"That was one reason." Damn it. Her heart had just managed to get back to a halfway normal rate and he had to go all smoldery on her. She needed to get her scrambled brains back in order. She was forgetting something important—

"Lucky for me, I was back here in the kitchen when I heard them come in. Even then, I barely had time to get out."

He'd gotten out in time, but what about the messages from Quinn? That's what she'd been forgetting. "Please, please tell me you took the messages from Quinn with you. Because they're not where I left them."

He dropped his hands from her face and reached under his sweatshirt, pulling out the manila envelope. "I did. But you shouldn't have kept these, Nicki. Today should have made that very clear."

He was right. Hadn't she told herself the same thing on her drive home? "I know."

She took the manila envelope and headed down the hall toward the front room. Dallas followed, sticking close enough that she could feel his nervous energy behind her. She put the envelope on the mantel and bent to pick up the fireplace lighter.

"You're going to burn them?" he asked quietly.

"Should have done it a long time ago." She put the envelope on the logs still lying in the hearth and touched the lighter flame to the edge. It caught fire and she set the lighter on the mantel.

She turned to look at Dallas. He was watching her movements, his dark-eyed gaze intense. "Are you okay? You're still sort of shivering. Come sit in front of the fire and tell me everything that happened."

He pulled up one of the chairs and sat in front of the hearth. The logs beneath the burning envelope had caught fire, the warming blaze impossible to resist. Nicki pulled up a chair as well and sat close to him, holding her hands out in front of the flames.

Something about Dallas had changed while she was gone. It wasn't anything big or obvious, just a subtle difference in the way he held himself. The way he spoke.

The way he looked at her.

Focus, Nicki.

She cleared her throat. "The men who came in here used a key, didn't they?"

"I think so. I heard what sounded like keys in

the lock. For a moment I thought it could be you, but it was too early."

"So they've made copies of my keys."

"Clearly."

She sighed. "Those sneaky bastards."

"You had to know it was a possibility. You're here as an undercover operative and you're trying to get inside their operation. They're going to give you a closer look, right? Maybe that's a good sign." The warmth of the fire seemed to be doing its job on Dallas. His earlier shivers had subsided, and his pale face had begun to take on a healthy color that she didn't think she could chalk up to the fire glow.

"It is a good sign," she agreed, remembering her own ordeal in the cave. "In fact, I think I know why they came here."

"You mean besides trying to see if you're up to something?"

"Well, that, obviously. What I mean is, there's a reason why they're doing it now."

"Something's changed, hasn't it?" He shot her a narrow-eyed look.

"Yeah. See, there's another reason I knew someone was here in my cabin. While I was picking up my message from the drop site, I heard people coming, so I hid. As it turned out, it was a good thing I did."

"Someone you knew?"

"Someone who may be key to getting me where I want to be on this assignment." She picked up the fire poker and gave the logs a nudge, igniting a shower of sparks. "His name is Del McClintock, and he's been my link to the people higher up in the BRI."

"Your link how?" The look Dallas slanted her way held an odd sort of vulnerability, as if her answer held a great deal of weight.

"Well, we're not sleeping together, if that's what you're asking."

"But you're seeing each other."

She sighed, leaning back in her chair. "It's complicated. We've been out a few times. Kissed a couple of times. I told him I was coming off a bad relationship and I didn't want to rush into anything."

"Kissed?"

Trust a man to latch on to that detail. "A couple of times. I think maybe it intrigues him—a woman who doesn't fall into his bed as soon as he looks her way."

"It can be very intriguing," Dallas agreed. "But how patient do you expect this guy to be?"

She sighed again. "Not very. But I'm not a little girl. I can handle myself with Del. And, apparently, what I'm doing is working better than I hoped."

He turned to look at her, his eyes narrowing. "Why do you say that?"

"Because when I was hiding from Del, I overheard him talking to another guy. And Del told that guy that his boss is very interested in me."

Dallas's brow creased. "What are you saying?"

"I'm saying, I think I'm finally going to get what I came here for. If I passed the test—I think that's what the search of my cabin must have been—they're going to hire me to be the man's medical caretaker." She smiled, torn between elation and sheer terror. "I'm about to find out who the head of the Virginia BRI really is."

Chapter Nine

Dallas took a step back, digesting Nicki's news with a sinking heart. Intellectually, he could acknowledge it was a significant turn of events in her investigation. He hadn't been on the front lines of the battle against the Blue Ridge Infantry and its attempt to build a complex and brutal crime syndicate in the guise of a homegrown militia, but anyone who worked at FBI headquarters knew what a coup it would be to position someone inside the group, feeding vital information to people with connections like Alexander Quinn had. He might be a civilian now, but Quinn still maintained a whole lot of ties to people inside the US justice system.

Nicki could be a real asset to the ongoing investigation.

She could also be embarking on a suicide mission.

"You might be getting into something you can't

get out of," he said finally when the silence between them began to grow tense.

She sighed. "I know. But it's what I came here to do. I knew going in it wasn't going to be a trip to the beach."

"You don't know all they're capable of. I don't even know what they're capable of, and I was their unwilling guest for weeks."

She put her hand on his arm, her fingers warm. "I know. But I've come this far. I have to see it through."

He wanted to shake off her hand, wanted to put distance between them as if he could somehow forestall the anxiety already rising in his gut like a poison tide. He knew more about what people like the BRI were capable of than she did. It hadn't taken captivity in their mountain enclave to acquaint him with that level of ruthlessness.

As bad as they were, the BRI wasn't that different from any gang of backwoods thugs out there. Sure, they'd upped their game by co-opting groups like the black bloc anarchists they'd brought into their fold, but they were still small-minded punks, no better than the meth cookers they had strong-armed into submission.

All the talk of patriotism and sovereign citizenship didn't change that fact.

"What are you thinking?" Nicki's voice was as warm as her touch, seductive without trying.

His resistance began to crumble under a swelling tide of desire.

He didn't dare tell her what he was really thinking. So he opted for what he'd been mulling before her touch had stoked a fire in his belly. "I was thinking the Blue Ridge Infantry isn't that different from people I grew up with back in Kentucky."

Her blue eyes narrowed slightly. "I suppose they're not. I've known a few like them myself. Back in Tennessee."

"They're mean. But they're also not nearly as smart as they think they are. I'm hoping we can use that against them."

She dropped her hand to her side. His arm felt cold where her hand had been, as if she'd taken all the warmth of the world with her. "I managed to leave the message for Quinn."

"How soon do you think your contact will show up?"

"I don't know," she admitted. Suddenly her eyes widened. "Oh. I forgot." She reached into the front pocket of her jeans and pulled out several folded sheets of paper. "Quinn had left me a message, but after I nearly ran into Del and his friend, I forgot all about it." She unfolded the papers and scanned them quickly, her brow furrowed.

"What is it?" Dallas asked.

"It's, um, just some notes." She darted a quick look at him.

"About me?"

She nodded. "Quinn isn't sure whose side you're on."

"And you're telling me that?"

Her gaze leveled with his. "I'm convinced you're on my side. If I weren't, I'd have told the boys from the BRI where to find you."

"Ruthless," he murmured, strangely unoffended.

"Would've earned me some points, don't you think?" She flashed him a quick smile that made his insides twist.

Maybe she was better prepared to deal with the BRI than he'd thought. "Anything else from Quinn?"

"He said to use my own judgment."

"He must trust you."

She gave a small shrug. "He knows my history. I take care of myself. I land on my feet."

"Your history?"

"It's a long story."

"One we have a little time for, since we're waiting on word from your boss about that computer equipment." He sat in the chair in front of the fire again and reached across to pat the empty chair beside him. "Come on. Story time. I'm too wired to sleep yet. How about you?"

Her lips quirked slightly as she gave him a side-eye look and sat in the chair next to him. "Only if you spill a little of your story, too."

He waved his hand dismissively. "Mine is dull. We'd be asleep in no time. You tell me your story instead. Once upon a time, there was a little girl named Nicki North—"

"Jamison."

He slanted a look at her. "Jamison North?"

Her lips quirked. "Nicki Jamison. Nicolette, actually."

"Pretty."

"Thank you. I had nothing to do with choosing it."

"Who did?"

She leaned her head back against the chair. "My mother. Andrea Jamison. She was just seventeen when I was born. I never knew my father, and, to be honest, I don't really believe any of the stories she told me about him."

"Why not?"

She closed her eyes. "Because one eighteen-year-old boy from Ridge County, Tennessee, can't be an astronaut, a guitar player in a rock band and the next Bill Gates all at the same time."

"Your mother dreamed big."

"She did." Nicki turned her head and opened her eyes. "Too big, sometimes."

"What does she think about your new assignment?"

Nicki's slight smile faded. "She died when I was sixteen. Drunk driving accident. She killed herself and a family of four after a few too many at the Whiskey Road Tavern."

He winced. "I'm sorry."

"She just couldn't get it together." She sighed. "Hell, most of the time, she didn't really try."

"What happened to you after that?"

"Nothing. I got myself declared an emancipated minor. I was already working afternoons at a diner in Bitterwood, and the owner, Maisey, let me live in a room over the diner until I graduated." Her smile was wistful, as if the memory was bittersweet. "Maisey offered to let me stay with her and her family, but I wanted out of Ridge County. So I left as soon as I could."

"Where'd you go?"

"Straight to hell in a handbasket." She laughed, but he didn't hear much amusement in her tone. "What about you? How'd you get from Kentucky to FBI headquarters?"

"By the skin of my teeth."

She nudged him with her elbow. "Are you trying to avoid my question, Mr. Cole?"

He was, a little. There was a lot in his past he'd

rather not remember, including how close he'd come to destroying his life.

"You *are* avoiding it, aren't you?"

"I just don't like to dwell on the past." The directness of her gaze was making him feel restless. He pushed to his feet and walked over to the window near the door. He opened the curtains a notch, just enough to look out on the moonlit yard without showing his face. He saw no signs of movement outside, but the earlier home invasion had left him feeling wary and restless.

"What happened out there?" Nicki asked, her voice closer than he anticipated.

He turned to look at her. She stood a couple of feet away, her head cocked with curiosity. The glow of firelight brought out glints of red in her dark hair and burnished her skin to a warm gold. "Out there?" he asked.

She closed the distance between them until she was only a few inches away. Close enough that he smelled the lingering scent of lemon-basil shampoo in her hair. "You seem—different." Her voice lowered a notch. "Dangerous."

He almost smiled at that notion, a rueful, humorless sort of smile that came from knowing just how close to the mark she was. There had been a time in his life when he had been on the cusp of being very dangerous indeed. A few steps in the wrong direction and he could have ended up like his brothers, venal and ruthless, carving out a truly wicked sort of life in the harsh Kentucky hill country.

He'd lied when he said there was no family left in Kentucky. There were his brothers. But he hadn't seen them in years.

By design.

"I'm a teddy bear," he said aloud.

She laughed. "No. You're not." She placed her hand flat against his breastbone, as if feeling for his heartbeat. His pulse leaped in response to her intimate touch, and he couldn't stop himself from leaning toward her.

"You're right. I can be very dangerous if I want to." He pressed his hand over hers, pinning it in place over his heart. "I've just tried really hard for a lot of years not to want to."

"But you want to now?" Her voice deepened. Softened.

His pulse rushed in his ears. "I don't want to. But I can if I'm forced to. That's what I remembered today. Out there."

Apparently, he still had a little bit of those unforgiving hills left inside him after all. And that piece of Kentucky might be his best hope of getting out of River's End alive.

Nicki touched his face, her fingers sliding across the stubble of beard with a soft rasp. "Have

I ever mentioned I have a soft spot for dangerous men?"

"No." He bent closer to her. "But I can't say
I'm surprised."

She rose to her toes, her mouth soft against
his. Sweet as mountain honey, darkened by the
razor edge of raw desire. He wrapped his arms
around her, pulling her closer, molding her body
against his until he felt utterly enveloped by her
soft heat. He explored the sleek contours of her
body, drawing a mental map of the endless possibilities of pleasure.

With his fingers he traced the arch of her
spine, sleeked along the dip of her waist and the
sweeping curve of her hips. A soft hum of pleasure rumbled from her throat, and he kissed her
there, along the taut tendon he found at the side
of her neck, drowning in the scent of her, the
silk of her.

She threaded her fingers through his hair and
dragged his face away, looking up at him with
passion-drunk eyes. "As much as I want this—
and believe me, I do—I don't think we should."

He wanted to argue. Almost did. But the harsh
crackle of the fire as a piece of burning log fell
into the embers made his nerves jerk, a potent re-
minder that for all the trappings of security the
cabin might offer, neither of them was truly safe.

This night was, at best, a brief respite in the fight for their lives yet to come.

And letting desire sweep them into mindless oblivion, however tempting a proposition, was pure folly.

They couldn't afford folly.

"You take the bed tonight," he suggested, moving a safe distance from where she remained, temptation incarnate, her desire-dark eyes and kiss-stung lips promising pleasures beyond imagination.

"You're still weak."

"No," he assured her. "I'm not."

Her eyes flickered at the raspy tone of his voice. "Okay. Try to get some sleep." She turned quickly and disappeared down the hall.

He almost followed. He actually took a few steps toward the doorway before he stopped himself, turning instead toward the sofa. The pillow and blankets she'd used the night before were nowhere to be found, he realized. She must have put them up this morning when she rose.

He found the bedding in the hall closet.

One door down from the bedroom.

He stared for a moment at the closed bedroom door, pressing the pillow and blankets tightly against his chest. He heard a whisper of movement beyond the door and pictured her readying herself for bed. Stripping out of her sweater and jeans, unfastening her bra to reveal the ripe curves of her breasts. Berry tipped, he thought. As sweet and lush as her lips.

He forced his feet to move back to the front room, nearly stumbling in his haste. He made up the sofa, stripped out of his sweatshirt and lay on his back on the sofa, gazing up at the play of light and shadows on the exposed beams of the ceiling.

She needs your help, he reminded himself. *And you need hers.*

DALLAS WAS AVOIDING HER. Not that he could really get very far away from her in the small cabin, but he somehow conspired to be in a different room as often as possible.

She aided his attempts at keeping his distance by taking double shifts at the diner for the next couple of days, partly to keep Trevor happy and partly in hopes of running into Del McClintock.

If the head of the Virginia BRI had really made the decision to take her on as a medical caretaker, shouldn't someone have approached her by now?

When her second shift ended without any sign of Del or any of the BRI boys at the diner, she started to worry. Maybe they'd found something at the cabin to give them pause, though she couldn't think what it could have been. She'd taken all of Dallas's dirty clothes and discarded them in a Dumpster the next town over that first day when she'd gone into town to work the morning shift. The only other incriminating things Ray and Craig could have found were her notes from Quinn and Dallas Cole himself.

What was the holdup?

She parked behind the hardware store again after her evening shift and hiked up the mountain to the drop site, not really expecting a message this early. But the signal was in place. Agent X had left her a message.

She retrieved the bundle of notes from the niche in the cave and scanned Quinn's message with the penlight on her key chain. The message was a brief set of directions that led her to a fallen pine tree fifty yards to the north of the cave. Under a canopy of pine boughs, she found a large backpack stashed out of sight.

Inside the pack was a new laptop computer and several pieces of equipment that she couldn't readily identify.

But Dallas Cole could, she was sure. He was the one who'd requested them.

She trekked down the mountain with the pack on her back, careful once she was out in the open to make sure she wasn't being watched. She stashed the backpack in the passenger floorboard and headed for the cabin.

As she slowed for the stop at Miller's Cross-roads, a loud horn blared behind her. Checking her rearview mirror, she saw Del McClintock's jacked-up Chevy Silverado idling behind her Jeep.

Damn it. If he saw the backpack and started asking questions—

The Silverado's driver's door opened and Del got out, heading for her Jeep.

She put the Jeep in Park and got out to meet him. "You scared the hell out of me, Del Mc-Clintock!" She softened her words with a smile.

He laughed. "I like to keep you on your toes, sugar!"

"Where've you been? I've been hoping to see you at the diner." She took another step closer to him, keeping him from getting too close to the Jeep. She touched the front of his jacket, fiddling with the zipper. "You don't like my cooking?"

"I love your cookin', sugar. You know that."

"You been out of town?"

"I had to go see somebody."

She flashed him a pouty look. "A girl?"

"No. It was business."

Her pulse quickened. "Anything good?"

"You might think so." He tugged at a lock of her hair. "How would you like to get away from that diner for a while? Work somewhere else?"

"Depends on where." She slid her hands teasingly up to his shoulders, swallowing her revulsion."

"I told you about my friend who's havin' trouble keepin' his diabetes under control, didn't I?"

"Right. You said he might need to go into the hospital for a while if he can't get his blood sugar regulated."

"He refuses to go to the hospital. His daddy went to the hospital a few years back with nothin' but a broken arm and died two days later. He won't go near a hospital."

"If he can't get his blood sugar under control, he'll end up there no matter what he wants," she warned, trying not to let her impatience show. Was he going to offer her the job or not?

"That's where you come in, sweetness." He stroked her cheek with the back of his hand. She tried not to react, but a faint shudder rippled through her. She had gotten bad at this game. There'd been a time when she could play the role of dutiful girlfriend without even blinking.

A lot had changed over the past few years. Herself included.

"He needs a personal nurse, I'd guess you'd say."

"I'm not a nurse," she said, hoping it wouldn't change his mind.

"You're close enough. You know how to administer his medication, right? Monitor his condition. Cook the kinds of meals he needs to eat to keep his sugar under control. Right?"

"I can do that," she agreed, excitement and dread fighting for control over her emotions.

"He wants to meet you. If he likes you, you're hired." Del grinned at her. "He pays really good, baby. And if you do a good job, he's gonna remember I'm the one who recommended you."

"Is that important?"

"It is." He pulled her into his arms and pressed his lips against her ear. "Real important."

That almost sounded like a threat, she realized.

She pulled back to look at him. "Then I'll be sure to do a good job."

He kissed her lightly. "I knew you would, sugar." He nodded at her idling Jeep. "You in a hurry to get home?"

"I have the morning shift, and I've just worked a double shift today. I'm beat. Rain check?"

"I'll hold you to it."

"When do I interview with your friend?"

He laughed softly. "Interview?"

"It's a job, right?"

"Yeah, it's a job." His smile faded. "You doing a double shift tomorrow?"

"No, I'm off at noon."

"I'll see if I can set something up for later in

the afternoon." He kissed her again, this time a longer, slower caress that made her skin crawl. "Call you tomorrow."

"I'll be expecting it." She pulled away from his embrace, flashed him a smile she hoped didn't look as sick as she felt and hurried back to the Jeep.

She hadn't stopped shaking by the time she reached the cabin, but she did her best to present a calm front when she carried the backpack of computer equipment inside where she found Dallas pacing by the fireplace.

He turned to look at her, his brow furrowed. "You're nearly an hour late."

She set the backpack on the coffee table and faced him. "I didn't know I was on a schedule," she snapped.

He shot her a disbelieving look. "You don't think I have a right to be concerned if you don't get back when I expect you to? Considering the kind of people you're rubbing elbows with?"

She wished elbows were all she'd rubbed with Del McClintock. She could still feel his hands on her back, his mouth on hers.

She felt dirty.

Dallas's expression shifted, his annoyance melting into concern as he crossed to her side. He put his hand on her cheek. "Are you okay?"

When he touched her, something inside her

broke, and she flung herself into his arms, burying her hot face in the curve of his neck. He wrapped his arms tightly around her, holding her close and murmuring nonsense against her temple.

After a moment, he cradled her face between his hands and made her look at him. "Did something happen?"

In answer, she rose to her toes and pressed her mouth against his, silencing his questions.

Chapter Ten

She tastes like fear.

The thought entered his overloaded brain and dug in its heels, refusing to budge, even as his body responded wildly to the feel of her slim, curvy body pressed intimately against his.

Her tongue tangled with his and all he could taste was the acid bite of fear. Her hands tugged the hem of his sweatshirt upward and slid along the flat planes of his abdomen, and he felt only the tremble of dread in her fingers.

He caught her hands and pulled away, gazing down into her too-bright eyes. "What happened?"

Her gaze dropped to his chest. "So much."

He led her over to the crackling fire, sat her in one of the chairs and crouched in front of her. "Start at the beginning. Why are you so late getting home?"

"I checked the dead drop and found Agent X

had left me directions to that." She waved her hand at the backpack she'd set on the coffee table.

"Agent X?" he asked as he crossed to the backpack.

She shot him a sheepish smile. "That's what I call him. I don't know his real name. I don't even know what he looks like."

He unzipped the main compartment. Inside, he found a laptop computer and accessories that matched the inventory of items he'd requested to the letter. "Quinn got his hands on this stuff very fast."

"That's Quinn," she said faintly.

He left the computer equipment where it sat, ignoring the itch to set it up and get started. Computer equipment hadn't sent unflappable Nicki Jamison into an anxiety attack. He crouched in front of her once more, ignoring the aches in his knees and back. "Why do I get the feeling that's not all that happened?"

"Because it's not," she admitted. "After I got the equipment, Del McClintock flagged me down at Miller's Crossroads."

The unease wriggling in Dallas's gut intensified. "Did he see the backpack?"

She shook her head. "I got out to meet him so he wouldn't see it."

"Then what happened?"

"I may have an interview tomorrow."

"An interview?"

"For a new job. Medical caretaker for a man with uncontrolled diabetes." She managed a bleak smile. "It's what I've been waiting to hear."

He laid his hands on her knees. "Then why do you look terrified?"

"Because I am?" She pushed his hands away and got up, walking to the window, then back to the mantel. "I don't know why Quinn thought I was the person to do this. Or, hell, maybe I do. Once an accomplished liar, always an accomplished liar, right?"

He caught her hand, stopping her nervous pacing. "If you don't want to do this, tell Quinn to find someone else."

"And throw away three months of setup right when it's about to pay off?" She shook her head firmly. "I've got a case of the nerves. That's all. It just came by surprise tonight and I wasn't prepared."

Just like that, her chin came up and her trembling subsided. A fierce light shone in her eyes, and he felt something turn flips in the center of his chest.

Damn, she was beautiful.

She nodded toward the backpack. "How quickly can you get that stuff set up?"

"Give me half an hour," he said, realizing he'd just been given marching orders. Tamping down the urge to argue her out of her plan of action, he gathered the items Quinn had provided for him to set up his own server and wireless connection, and got to work.

Within thirty minutes, the sea of gadgets and wires inside the pockets of the backpack combined with the high-powered smartphone Quinn supplied had transformed into a working internet system under his hands. He showed Nicki the search engine browser page with a smile of triumph. "We're in business."

"Yay?"

"Technophobe," he muttered with a laugh. "I don't know how you lived here three days without the internet, much less three months."

"You do know that Quinn has probably set up something that'll monitor whatever you do on that server, don't you?"

He looked up, surprised by her serious tone. "Is that how he does business?"

"Former CIA," she said, as if that explained everything.

Probably did, he conceded. "I'll check everything out." There were a few ways Quinn could have set up tracking software and a few other tricks that the average computer user would never find.

But Dallas wasn't the average computer user.

"I might be up a few more hours." He looked at her, noting the faint shadows of weariness beneath her eyes. "Go to bed. Get some sleep. Don't you have a morning shift?"

"I do," she agreed with a slight smile. "You sure you don't want to save this until morning?"

"Positive. Take the bed again. I'll bunk down here once I'm done."

She didn't move right away, her blue eyes holding his gaze for a long, heated moment. "Thank you."

"For what?"

"For making me feel less alone." She flashed him a twitch of a smile, then turned and left the room quickly.

He released a long, slow breath, quelling the powerful urge to put the computer aside and follow her back to the bedroom.

Focus, Cole.

He examined some of the more obvious places Quinn and his computer people might have hidden a keystroke logger in the system and found nothing. Digging deeper, however, he discovered a program he was pretty sure had been designed to track anything he did on the computer.

Removing it would be easy enough, but he'd never been one to do the easy thing.

Instead, he recoded the program slightly, ensuring that anything sent to Quinn would be gibberish.

Ought to make his point, he thought.

After another hour examining the ins and outs of the system, he'd found one more tracking program, quickly dispatched, then settled down to work.

Before leaving for work that afternoon, Nicki had given him a list of names she'd gleaned during her time in River's End. Del McClintock was the first on the list, and he began there.

A simple internet search came up with nothing of interest, but internet searches were child's play. Everybody had a footprint. The key was figuring out where to look. And one of the most useful things he'd learned in the cybersecurity classes he'd taken over the past couple of years with the FBI was exactly where to look.

GUILT TASTED LIKE ASHES, *smoky and bitter. The flavor burned her nose and brought stinging tears to her eyes that spilled down her cheeks in hot streaks.*

She'd done her job. The Tennessee Bureau of Investigation had acted on the tip she'd given them, the tip she'd gotten from Jeff Burwell.

Now she had to figure out how to say goodbye to Jeff and the kids without telling them the truth—she'd never been just their housekeeper.

She'd been a spy, taking advantage of the family's vulnerability to find out what the Blue Ridge

Infantry was up to in the little town of Thurlow Gap, Tennessee.

"They're not going to know who gave us the information," her handler, Martin Friedman, had assured her earlier that day when they'd met at a truck stop out of town. "You can stick around the farm another two or three weeks, just so nobody gets suspicious, then turn in your notice."

"Then what?" she'd asked, feeling strangely empty.

"Then we'll find a new assignment for you. You've been a big asset. The higher-ups won't forget it."

She should have felt pleased with herself. The TBI certainly seemed to be pleased with her.

But all she'd felt was sick.

The farmhouse was quiet. Jeff was in town visiting his mother, who'd been feeling poorly for the past few days. The kids were asleep upstairs in their bedrooms. Nicki had been trying to read for an hour, but her mind kept wandering back to the choices she'd made in the past few months.

She could almost smell the ashes of regret.

She sat up straighter, opening her eyes.

That wasn't regret.

That was fire.

The darkness outside had taken on an eerie glow. She hurried to the closest window and pushed aside the curtain, her heart skipping a *beat as she saw flames edging close to the house, the edges blurred by a miasma of thick smoke.*

The winter had been dry. Too dry.

As she started toward the stairs, the front door opened and Jeff Burwell rushed inside, his dark eyes wild and his face and clothes smudged with soot.

"The house is on fire!" he shouted, pushing past her up the stairs.

Her knees buckled beneath her, and she grabbed for the back of the rocker, her heart pounding with dread.

"Nicki!" Jeff called from the top of the stairs.

But flames rose up, surrounding her.

Scorching her.

It took a moment to realize the fire came from inside her own body.

"Nicki?"

Nicki woke with a cry, bolting upright in the bed, her galloping pulse thundering in her head.

The bed shifted beside her, and strong arms wrapped around her body, pulling her close. "It's okay," Dallas's voice rumbled in her ear. "It's just a dream."

She pressed her forehead in the curve of his neck, gulping deep breaths until her heart rate settled down to a canter. "It wasn't a dream."

"Yes, it was. Everything's okay." He threaded his fingers through her hair, drawing her head back until she was gazing up at him in the dim half-light of the bedroom. Light filtered in from the front of the house, obscuring half of his face in shadow, but the determined look in his dark eyes was unmistakable.

Her knight in shining armor, she thought, swallowing a smile.

Who said they didn't exist?

"I'm okay," she assured him, but he didn't let her go, his thumbs drawing soothing circles on either side of her chin.

"You were moaning. I heard you all the way down the hall."

"Like you said, just a dream." His touch felt like a brand, burning all the way to her soul, the intensity of sensation reminding her strangely of her dream and the feeling that the fire that effectively destroyed Jeff Burwell's life had started somewhere inside her.

She pulled away, rising from the bed and crossing to the window. For a moment, the world outside seemed to be on fire, as if an afterimage of her dream lingered. But the mirage of hazy flames subsided, leaving behind only the moonlit winter woods.

"You said it wasn't a dream. What did you mean?"

She sighed. "Nothing. I guess I wasn't quite awake yet."

"Come on, Nicki. It wasn't nothing."

"I was just dreaming about the fire." She turned to look at him. "The one in Tennessee."

"When you were working for the TBI?"

She nodded. "I'd just met with my handler and he'd told me the job was done. They'd thwarted the plot against the conservation officers and I could leave the Burwell farm soon."

"You'd saved lives."

"I'd betrayed people who trusted me." She turned back to the window, remembering her encounter with Del McClintock. "It seems to be what I'm good at."

"Are you regretting your choice to come here?"

She shook her head. "No. Del McClintock isn't Jeff Burwell. He's a very bad guy with very bad intentions. All of those men I'm dealing with these days deserve everything they get."

"But there's something still troubling you."

She pressed her forehead against the cold windowpane. "They have families. Wives and women. Kids. Most of those women depend entirely on their men for their sustenance. Some of them can barely read and write. Not many of them have job skills that would give them a chance to get the hell out of this place and make a better life for themselves and their kids."

"So you're supposed to just let their men get away with murder?"

"Of course not." Her breath had made a foggy patch of condensation on the window. She lifted her fingers and wiped it away. "There just aren't any winners here."

She felt him walk up behind her, his body a comforting wall of heat against her back. He wrapped his arms around her and rested his cheek against her temple. "No, I guess there aren't."

She leaned back against him, taking comfort in his closeness. The sense of vulnerability should have scared her, but it didn't. It felt...right.

Now *that* scared her. But not enough to compel her to move away.

"How's Operation Computer Geek going out there?"

"All set up."

She glanced at her watch. It was only a little after midnight. She'd figure he'd be up for hours getting the system going. "That's fast."

"Not really. Want to see it at work?"

Part of her did. But the other part wanted to stay right where she was, safely wrapped in his warm embrace. She went with that part. "Maybe in the morning."

"Just so you know, I've set it up so that it's easily hidden in a matter of seconds. I can show you tomorrow, in case you ever have to stash it away quickly."

That was good thinking, she realized, considering their recent home invasion. "Are you sure it's something a techno-troglodyte like me can handle?"

He laughed in her ear. "Yes."

They fell silent as they gazed out the window at the woods, their breathing settling into harmony until she had the strangest feeling that she couldn't tell where her body ended and his began.

When a sharp pounding noise from the front of the house shattered the silent communion, it rattled her all the way to her bones.

Her heart instantly racing again, she jerked free of his grasp and turned to look at him. "That's someone at the door. You need to hide. Now."

"I've got to get the computer equipment."

Damn it. "Fine. Then you hide."

The banging noise continued as she led him into the front room. "Make it quick," she whispered, but he was already disengaging cords and packing equipment into the backpack from which it had come.

"Hide where?" he whispered as he zipped the bag.

"The cellar."

He shot her an odd look, drawing heat to her cheeks as she remembered his last visit to her cellar. But he slung the backpack over his shoulder and disappeared down the hall.

The pounding on the door grew louder. "Nicki!"

The voice on the other side belonged to Keith Pickett. He sounded drunk and scared.

"Coming!" she called, listening for the sound of the cellar door shutting. When she heard the soft click, she hurried to the door and turned the key in the lock.

Keith stood outside, looking pale and sick. His eyes were bloodshot and there was blood on his jeans.

A lot of blood.

"I think I've killed her," he said, his voice slurred and pitiful.

Nicki's heart skipped a beat. "Kaylie?"

"She's bleedin' all over the place. I didn't even hit her that hard."

"Where is she?" Her sluggish brain tried to catch up, tried to gather up all the scattered pieces of her thoughts into something coherent. She needed supplies, to start with. The first-aid kit in her bathroom would have to do.

"She's out in the truck!"

She stared at him in horror. "You drove her here?"

"She's dyin' and she kept sayin' you'd know what to do."

It was a miracle they'd made it up the mountain road alive, as drunk as Keith was. "Stay right here—let me get my kit."

She hurried back to the bathroom, taking a

quick look around as she went to make sure she and Dallas hadn't left anything incriminating in the den. Her heart skipped a beat when she realized the extra pillow and blankets were out on the sofa, but she shoved the worry aside. He was drunk and probably wouldn't remember much of this night at all by morning.

She grabbed her kit and followed Keith's weaving path out to his battered Chevy Tahoe. The passenger door was open and Kaylie was bent forward, vomiting on the gravel.

Keith hadn't been lying. There was a lot of blood, staining the lap of her cotton housedress and spilling down her legs onto the truck's running board.

Her face was bruised, her lip bloodied. The son of a bitch had been hitting her.

"Did you hit her in the stomach?" she growled at Keith.

"No, I swear I didn't."

"He didn't," Kaylie growled between heaves. Nothing was coming out now but she couldn't seem to stop retching.

There was no choice. She pulled out her phone and dialed 911.

Keith grabbed her arm, trying to pull the phone away. "What the hell are you doin'?"

She jerked her arm free. "Saving her life. And keeping your ass off death row." She heard the dispatcher answer and quickly gave her address. "I have an injured, pregnant woman in trouble," she said, her gaze drawn to the puddle of blood pooling on the gravel beneath Kaylie's feet. Her heart sank to the pit of her stomach as she opened her kit and pulled out a pair of surgical gloves. "Get an ambulance here, stat!"

Chapter Eleven

The sirens had come and gone, and above Dallas's hiding place in the cellar, the house had grown silent. Without a watch or any way to gauge the passage of time, he was beginning to grow restless and panicked.

The frantic sound of a man's voice had carried all the way down to the cellar, but whoever had been banging on the front door had retreated moments later, and all had been silent for a long while.

Then came the sirens. They'd died away for a few minutes, then fired up again and began to fade into the distance.

And still, he waited.

He was certain more than an hour had passed before he finally heard the sound of footsteps on the floorboards overhead. Slow, deliberate steps moving closer until he heard the cellar door rattle open.

"You can come up." Nicki's voice sounded hoarse and tired.

He climbed the steps, meeting her at the top. She leaned against the wall across from him, purple shadows bruising the skin under her eyes. There was blood streaked on her jeans and the hem of her sweater, and her arms from the wrists up were similarly stained.

He looked her over, trying to find the source of the blood, but she didn't seem to be injured. "Are you okay?" he asked, his heart thumping painfully against his sternum.

She looked down at her red-stained arms. "I need a shower."

"Whose blood is that?"

"A woman I know. She was pregnant."

"Was?"

"I don't know if she still is. I don't see how she could be." She walked down the hall to the bathroom and entered, leaving the door open.

He followed, standing in the doorway as she turned on the tap and washed her arms in the sink. "Miscarriage?"

"Of a sort."

"What does that mean?"

She soaped her skin up to her elbows liberally, the suds turning pink as they dripped into the sink. "Her man hits her. He didn't admit it, but I think he hit her in the abdomen tonight."

"Bastard."

She nodded solemnly. "That's the sheriff's problem now."

"I heard sirens."

"That was the ambulance. The deputies came in lights on but siren off." She rinsed off the soap and examined her arms closely, frowning. She grabbed the soap and lathered up again.

"The last thing you needed, huh? The cops nosing around?"

She rinsed off the soap again. "I'm hoping they won't hold it against me. It's not like I asked to be involved in this mess."

"Why'd they come to you?"

"I told you, I took pains to build myself a reputation as the go-to person when someone in the BRI had a medical issue."

He frowned at her bleak tone. "Were you able to do something for her?"

"I kept her from going into shock. I kept her calm. But a uterine hemorrhage is beyond my ability to stop outside of a hospital." She examined her arms again and apparently found them satisfactory. She wiped them dry on a hand towel hanging nearby and turned to look at him. "This isn't about me or this case. That son of a bitch knew she was pregnant. He got her that way, and then he took it from her." Her lips were trembling, and her jaw was tight with rage.

"I take it this isn't your first time dealing with them?"

"I've been trying to help some of the women." She pushed past him into the hall, then through to her bedroom. "Sometimes I think it's a lost cause. Nobody respects them as valuable human beings. Not even themselves." She opened one of her dresser drawers and pulled out a change of clothes. "Some of them barely know how to read or write. Some are hooked on meth or heroin. They have babies who are born with drug habits."

"Poverty is brutal."

"It's not just poverty. It's these people. These sick, violent, power-hungry bastards called the Blue Ridge Infantry." She slammed the dresser drawer shut, making the mirror rattle against the wall. "I've known people in militias before. Some of them honestly wanted to be prepared to defend themselves in the case of some sort of foreign invasion. Some were just idiots with guns looking for a reason to play soldier. But the BRI is different. They're criminals who try to excuse their crimes under the guise of patriotism. They make me sick."

"Tell me what I can do," he said quietly.

She stopped in the middle of picking up her clothes and looked at him, as if startled by his tone. "There's nothing you can do."

"I'm not talking about the BRI. I'm talking about you. What can I do for you?"

Her lips trembled, and she shook her head. "I'm okay."

He didn't believe her. When she reached for the clothes again, he caught her hand and tugged her to him, wrapping his arms around her.

She resisted a moment. "You'll get blood on your clothes."

He didn't let her go. "It'll wash out."

She relaxed against him, resting her temple against his chin. Her breath was warm on his collarbone. "I don't know if this will affect their plans for me. I hope it won't, but I may have to work at this a little longer, regain some of their trust."

"Because you tried to help one of their women?"

"Because I called paramedics for help. They really don't want to get any sort of authorities involved. And the paramedics called the sheriff's department."

"Which means the big bad bully has to answer to the law?"

"Also not a good thing."

"Did you lie to the deputies?"

Her voice came out low and tight. "No. I told them everything I knew about the things that bastard has done to Kaylie since I've been in

River's End. Maybe I shouldn't have played it that way, but—"

"Good for you. Being undercover shouldn't have to mean selling your soul." He cradled her face between his hands. "Go take a shower. I'll make sure everything's secure for the night."

He took his time, making sure the cabin was locked up tight while she showered off the rest of the blood. As he was looking around, he scouted a new place to keep his computer equipment, since tonight's surprise visit had made it clear that the front room was far too exposed to be a good choice.

Besides the front room, the small cabin had four other rooms—the bathroom, the kitchen, Nicki's bedroom and a tiny room that she seemed to use as a storage area. He was still looking around the small room, gauging its utility as a computer room, when Nicki came out of the shower and found him there.

She'd changed into a pair of slim-fitting yoga pants and a long-sleeved T-shirt, her feet encased in a thick pair of socks and her wet hair turbaned in a towel. "What are you looking for?"

He told her. "I think we could stack a few boxes in the corner there and make room for some sort of desk here near the window. It should allow for decent cell phone reception, which I'll need for the internet."

"Del said he'd try to set up an interview for me later in the afternoon. He'll call to let me know. But I think that'll give me time to pick up a desk at the thrift store in Abingdon before the interview." She looked him over with a bemused half smile. "I could pick up some clothing for you, too."

He looked down at his mismatched, borrowed clothes. "That would be welcome," he admitted. "But are you sure you'll have time?"

"I'll make time," she said firmly. "I'll need you to feed me information once I get deeper into the operation, so it's in my best interest to get your computer set up and working."

"Are they going to expect you to give up your cabin?"

"I'm sure I'll be moving in with the patient to give him twenty-four-hour care."

"So people will expect the place to be empty." He frowned.

"It's so far off the beaten track, I'm not sure there'd be anyone around to notice if it's occupied," she said. "Not that it matters. I rent the place, anyway, so if I leave, they'll just figure someone else rented it."

"What about your landlord? Won't he or she ask questions?"

She smiled. "My landlord is Alexander Quinn, actually. Though this place can't be traced back to him easily. So you can remain here to do your computer magic while I'm gone."

His gut twisted a little. Gone seemed such a final word. "Are you sure this is a good idea?"

Her brow furrowed. "Your staying here?"

"No. Your going there."

"Oh." Her smile faded. "I don't know if I'd call it a good idea, no. But it's necessary. And I'm in the best position to do it."

"Assuming what happened tonight doesn't change their plans."

She nodded. "Assuming that."

"You look tired. You should get some sleep. I'll go fetch the computer stuff I left in the cellar. I think there might be an old table down there I can use until you have a chance to pick up a desk at the thrift store." He started past her, then stopped, touching her cheek with his fingertips. "I hope your friend is okay. When will you find out?"

"I don't know. Probably when I get to work in the morning. Small town. News travels fast." She touched his hand where it lay against her cheek, giving it a light squeeze. "Thank you. I'm not sure what I'd have done if you hadn't been here tonight."

"You'd have done exactly what you did," he said with certainty. There was a reason a man like Alexander Quinn chose Nicki Jamison to take on the job of getting inside the Blue Ridge

Infantry when none of his male operatives had been able to pull it off.

And it wasn't just her pretty face or killer curves.

Impulsively, he kissed her forehead, his lips smoothing over the furrows he felt forming there. "Good night." He left the room while he still could and headed down to the cellar to gather his computer equipment.

By the time he'd carried everything up to the spare room, including the battered wood work-table he planned to use as a desk, Nicki had disappeared into her bedroom and closed the door. Taking care not to make a lot of noise that might wake her, Dallas set up the equipment again and got to work making a to-do list of things he wanted to accomplish with his newly regained access to the internet.

He had started a cursory search for information about Del McClintock before Nicki's nightmare had interrupted him. He hadn't gotten very far, though he'd found a promising entry in a list of Virginia National Guard members involved in a counterdrug program. A Delbert McClintock had been part of the program in southwestern Virginia.

He made a note to look deeper the next day. But he had another priority at the moment.

His own access to the FBI's network would

have been cut off by now, but he knew where the back doors were in the system. If he played his cards right, took care not to leave a footprint, there was a chance he could sneak all the way to the top of the food chain.

Well, almost the top. Assistant Director Philip Crandall hadn't made it to the top spot yet.

But taking down an assistant director would take more than the word of a disgraced FBI support staffer.

Dallas needed proof. Hard evidence that Crandall had an agenda that had nothing to do with bringing the Blue Ridge Infantry to justice.

And time was running out.

DEL MCCLINTOCK HADN'T called Nicki by the time she finished her morning shift at the diner. In fact, none of the BRI boys showed up at the diner at all, a fact that made Nicki more nervous than she liked to admit.

But news of Kaylie Pickett's misfortune was already making the rounds on the River's End grapevine. Descriptions of her condition varied from critical to stable, but everyone agreed that Keith Pickett had caused her injury and Nicki had saved her life.

"You're a hero," Bella told her in a hushed tone, her eyes wide with admiration that made

Nicki feel a little uncomfortable. "I heard she was bleeding to death and you stopped it."

"I just called an ambulance and kept her warm and as calm as I could," Nicki said, trying to cut off any further discussion. The last thing she wanted to be was the center of attention. It was a sure way to put a target on her back. "It's too bad about the baby."

"Oh. You didn't hear?" Bella lowered her voice. "She didn't lose the baby."

Nicki stared at her. "That's not possible."

"I heard the doctor said the same thing. But that little fella was still hanging in there last I heard."

Bella must have heard wrong, Nicki thought. She'd seen the amount of blood, the condition Kaylie had been in by the time the ambulance arrived. The grapevine must have this part wrong.

But, as it turned out, Nicki was wrong. The diner phone rang shortly before eleven, as she was helping Bella and Trevor clean up after most of the breakfast crowd had cleared out but before the lunch crowd started to wander in. Trevor went to answer it and came back with a frown on his face. He looked pointedly at Nicki. "Del McClintock. Wants to talk to you."

She went very still, her pulse suddenly pounding in her ears. Forcing her feet into motion, she walked back to the break room and picked up the phone. "Hi, Del."

"I hear tell you're a hero."

She glanced at Trevor, who had followed her down the hall and stood in the doorway, watching her with a troubled expression. Turning her back, she lowered her voice. "I think that's a bit of an exaggeration."

"You saved Kaylie Pickett and her baby. That's pretty big, I'd say."

"So the baby really did make it."

"He did."

"It's a boy?"

"That's what Kaylie said the doctor told her. Says she's going to name him Nick. After you."

To her surprise and mortification, hot tears welled in her eyes. She pushed them away with her knuckles. "Tough little fellow. I never would've thought he'd make it."

"Kaylie's gotta be real careful for the next couple of months. But the doctor thinks she's got a real good chance of that baby comin' out just fine."

"Amazing."

"That's what I said when I told my friend about what you'd done." Del sounded satisfied. "He was very impressed. In fact, I think the word he used for you was 'gutsy.'"

"I'm surprised you and your buddies aren't

slamming me for telling the law what Keith did to Kaylie."

Del's tone was dismissive. "Keith's an idiot. And a brute. Not everybody thinks women are punchin' bags, you know."

"Enough do."

"We're workin' on that," Del said.

Nicki knew better than to believe him. She'd heard the way he talked to—and about—women when he didn't know she was listening. He was putting on an act for her because he needed her as much as she needed him.

She was as much his "in" with the top guy as he was hers, she suspected.

"He wants to meet you, but he can't do it today. How about tomorrow?"

She suppressed a sigh of frustration. Waiting another day wouldn't kill her, but patience wasn't one of her virtues. "Okay. Tomorrow's great. Any particular time?"

"What's your work schedule?"

"I'm off Fridays."

"Great. I'll pick you up around eleven and we'll go meet your new employer."

"Don't jump the gun," she said, trying not to sound as nervous as she felt. "He may hate me."

"Impossible, sugar."

"Listen, why don't we just meet at the diner so you don't have to come all the way out to my place?" The last thing she could afford was Del finding out she had Dallas Cole stashed at her cabin.

"If you want." Del lowered his voice, as if he didn't want to be heard on his end of the line. "I have tonight free. Want to drive into Abingdon with me for dinner?"

She frowned. Del had never asked her out on a formal date before. "I've let my cabin get in terrible shape this week, so I really need to stay home and clean. Maybe tomorrow after we talk to your friend? Maybe we can make it a celebration."

"It will be."

"It's a date," she said with as much warmth as she could muster. She hung up and turned around to see Trevor still watching her.

"What?" she asked Trevor.

"Del McClintock isn't a nice guy."

"Maybe I'm not lookin' for a nice guy."

"Nicki—"

"I know what I'm doing, Trevor." She met his gaze without flinching. "I know exactly what I'm doing." She untied her apron and tossed it in the laundry bin near the break room door. "I'll come in early Saturday, but I'm leavin' for today." She walked out past him, her head held high.

Outside, the day was mild, with plenty of warm sunshine to drive away the slight morning chill. Spring would be here soon. She had a feeling it would be a pretty season in this part of the Blue Ridge Mountains. It always had been one of her favorite times of year back home in the Tennessee Smokies.

She slid behind the wheel of the Jeep and pulled out her cell phone. Calling information, she got the number of the hospital in Abingdon and called to see if Kaylie was still a patient there. To Nicki's surprise, she'd already been released.

She'd drop by later to check on her, she decided. But first, she needed to make a run to the thrift store in Abingdon.

An hour later, she had a bag full of used clothes for Dallas, but she'd had no luck finding a desk. The worktable would have to do a little while longer, she supposed.

Before she'd left that morning, she and Dallas had worked out a knock signal. Three sharp raps meant everything was okay. If she entered without knocking, he was to bug out as fast as he could.

She parked in front of the cabin and climbed the stairs, giving three sharp raps on the door before she entered. She half expected to hear the clatter of the laptop keyboard coming from down the hall, so the silent stillness that greeted her caught her off guard.

The storage room was empty, though Dallas's computer setup was still there, out in the open.

She continued to the kitchen, where she found him sitting at the table, reading what looked like a letter.

He looked up when she entered, waving for her to sit at the table with him.

She put the bag of clothes in the empty chair next to him. "Got you a few clothes, but I didn't find a desk yet."

"Thanks." He flashed her a strained smile that quickly faded. "How was your shift?"

"The usual," she said. "Del called before I left."

"Is the meeting with your potential patient still on?"

"Tomorrow afternoon." She nodded at the letter. "What's that?"

"A message from your boss. I found it on the hard drive when I got in there and started looking around. He was kind enough to include a small printer in the setup, so I printed it out." He handed it to her.

She scanned the note quickly, recognizing Quinn's terse tone. She reached the end and read it again, her gut tightening. "This is crazy."

Dallas nodded, looking grim. "I know."

"This Michelle Matsumara—she was your boss at the FBI, right?"

"Right." His voice came out low and strangled.

"And now they think you killed her?"

He looked up, tears in his eyes. "Maybe I did."

Chapter Twelve

"You didn't kill her."

Dallas looked up at Nicki as she rose from her chair, flattened her palms against the table and leaned over him, her expression fierce. Not for the first time, she reminded him of some sort of fabled warrior princess, her eyes flashing blue fire and her jaw squared with determination.

He was lucky she was an ally, not an enemy.

"I didn't mean it literally." He slumped back against the chair and regarded her, acutely aware that by coming here, he may have put her in Philip Crandall's crosshairs, as well. "But she was killed because of me. Because of the choices I made."

"You don't know that."

"Don't I?"

"Have you even looked for the story online? Or did you read that note from Quinn and immediately start beating yourself up?"

He glared at her. "I looked it up."

"What happened to her?"

"The police have been tight-lipped, but the speculation is that she surprised an intruder."

"Maybe that's really what happened."

"There's a reason the police are looking for me for questioning. Don't you think?" He pushed up from his chair and paced to the window, gazing out past the curtains at the small backyard. Sunlight dappled the ground, filtering through evergreens that towered over the small cabin. The day looked mild, the first mild day in a week.

He suddenly felt trapped, a prisoner to his own choices.

"I should turn myself in," he said aloud.

Behind him, Nicki remained silent. But he felt her tension.

"I'm putting you in danger by being here," he added, turning to look at her. "I'm certainly not making your assignment any easier."

"If you turn yourself in, you'll be a sitting duck," she warned. "A man like Philip Crandall can make things happen, even in the jailhouse."

"At least he wouldn't be trying to get to me through other people."

"So you let him win? You fall on your own sword and make it easier for him to keep doing whatever it is he's doing?" She shook her head. "That's cowardice. And I don't think you're a coward."

Anger welled inside him. Anger and a gnawing, grating pain that seemed to be shredding his insides, inch by inch. "I don't understand why he went after Michelle. Why her? She was so decent. Funny and good-natured and so very, very decent." Tears burned his eyes, but he fought them. Fought the weakness they represented.

He could mourn later. Right now, Michelle needed his vengeance, not his grief.

Nicki pulled the chair up next to him and took his hands in hers. "Tell me about her."

He shook his head. "I don't need to talk it out."

"Tell me about her, anyway. I want her to be real to me."

He looked up and found her eyes blazing at him again. "Why?"

Her grip on his hands tightened. "Because I want her in my head when I help take those sons of bitches down."

He lifted her hands to his lips and kissed her knuckles. "You'd have liked her."

"So tell me about her," she said again. "Was she married?"

"Divorced. Married young, right out of college. She never talked badly of him, but I got the feeling he wasn't exactly the faithful sort."

"Any children?"

"No. She had two cats she treated like they were her children." He frowned. "I wonder what'll happen to them."

"I'm sure someone will take them. Did she have family around?"

"No. They lived in San Francisco. All the way across the country." It was stupid, he thought, that of all the things he should be worrying about, all he could think about was those two silly cats of hers. "You don't think they'll take those cats to a shelter, do you?"

"I don't know. I could get a message to Quinn, see what he could do. He probably knows people who could make sure they get a good home."

He squeezed her hands. "You think I'm being foolish."

"No, I don't. I think you're grieving a friend. And however you need to do that is okay."

"I wish—" He broke off, not sure what he wished. That Michelle was still alive? Of course he wished that. He wished he'd never gotten that second call from Cade Landry. He'd be at his office in DC right now, putting together a brochure or creating new graphics for the next recruiting pamphlet.

He wouldn't be sitting in a cabin in the Blue Ridge Mountains, holding hands with an undercover operative and missing the hell out of a woman who hadn't deserved to die so young.

"Did she have any reason to suspect Philip Crandall was behind your disappearance?" Nicki asked a few minutes later.

"I don't know. She was smart. But she didn't know I went to Crandall about Cade Landry. I didn't suspect anything about Crandall myself until I spoke to him directly."

"Did he say something to make you suspicious?"

"Just that he wanted me to keep silent about it. Not tell anyone else that Cade Landry had called me."

Her eyes narrowed. "That doesn't sound unreasonable."

"It wasn't, I suppose."

"But it made you suspicious, anyway."

"You ever had that little voice in the back of your head that says 'something's not right here'?"

She nodded.

"That's what I heard. Something wasn't right." He brushed his thumb over the back of her hand, knowing he should let go. Put more distance between them rather than cling to her as if she was his only lifeline.

But he couldn't seem to do it. It felt as if there was a part of him that would shatter if he let go. And as much as that notion should scare him, it didn't. It made him feel steadier somehow. Needing another person—needing her—wasn't a sign of weakness.

It was a show of strength.

"You're sure it was Crandall who sicced those guys on you? The ones who ran you off the road?"

"I didn't tell anyone else my suspicions about Crandall. Nobody but Cade Landry and Olivia Sharp. You know Olivia, right? I mean, since she also works for The Gates."

"I know her."

"Anyway, by that time, I was already being followed."

"Could someone have intercepted the call from Landry?"

"Maybe. But I'm not exactly someone they'd have thought to put under surveillance, especially after the last time."

"The last time?"

He looked down at their entwined hands. "You know Cade Landry disappeared almost a year ago, don't you? Long before he resurfaced again earlier this year."

"Right. The FBI suspected him of being involved in a plot to kill one of their undercover operatives."

"He knew he was a suspect, and he had some information to share with Assistant Director Crandall, but he didn't want to go through normal channels. So he called me."

"Why you? You're not an agent."

"I think that's probably why," he answered with

a smile. "I'm nobody. Who'd suspect that I'd get a call from a rogue agent?"

"How did Landry even know you?"

"He went through a cybersecurity course the same time I did a little over a year ago. He was being moved to an RA—Resident Agency—down in Tennessee and they wanted him to be their point man on cybersecurity. I guess he remembered me when he needed help."

"You didn't suspect Crandall the first time you went to him?"

"I didn't go to him," Dallas answered quietly, letting go of her hands and sitting back.

"But you said Landry asked you to bypass channels."

"I didn't listen to him. I thought he was being paranoid. The rules were there for a reason. The chain of command isn't just some arbitrary set of standards."

"And that's when things went wrong for Landry."

"From what I've heard, he disappeared overnight. All his stuff was gone from his apartment and a lot of people thought he'd just run off."

"But he hadn't."

"No. I never thought he had. I knew from the scuttlebutt at the Bureau that the brass thought Landry had been corrupted by the Blue Ridge Infantry and their criminal cohort. Do you remember hearing about those two bombers who blew up a warehouse in Virginia a few years ago?"

She nodded. "I was doing some work for the Nashville police then. Everybody was on edge, wondering if we were about to see a bunch of those small-scale terror attacks from the likes of the Blue Ridge Infantry or maybe some low-level copycats. Everyone was on high alert."

"Landry was on the FBI SWAT team that went after those guys. He and his team went in early, against orders, although he swears he got an order to go in. Two of the men on his team were killed. It basically ruined his career."

"The FBI thought he botched the raid on purpose?"

"They weren't sure. They couldn't prove anything obviously, or they'd have charged him."

"So when he suddenly went missing in the middle of an investigation of the Blue Ridge Infantry—"

"A lot people figured he'd gone over to the dark side for good," he finished for her.

"What about you? What did you think?"

"I thought he was dead." He stood up. "But clearly he wasn't. And when I heard from him again, I decided to do things his way."

"Which still didn't work the way he hoped?" She stood, as well.

"You tell me. I thought he was dead until you

told me he's not." He nodded toward the hallway. "Sitting here wallowing in regret isn't going to stop Crandall. I need to figure out more about what's going on with the BRI. Especially if you're about to come face-to-face with their top man."

She followed him to the spare room and stood in the door, watching while he pulled up a chair to the worktable holding his computer. "Do you really think you can get that kind of information on the internet? I'm pretty sure there are loads of people, civilians and lawmen alike, trying to get that kind of information. And nobody's had any luck so far."

"That's because they're looking in the wrong places," he said.

"And you think you know the right places to look?" She sounded skeptical.

He shot her a cocky look, taking masculine satisfaction in the rush of color that stained her cheeks in response. "I guess we're about to find out."

"Sir, you asked me to inform you of anything that might be an attempted intrusion."

Assistant Director Philip Crandall looked up from his paperwork and found Hopkins from the cybersecurity section. He waved the woman in. "You've found something?"

"I believe so," she answered, a frown etching

thin lines in her pale forehead. Jessica Hopkins was a tall, slim woman in her late twenties who looked a decade younger, thanks to good skin and her apparent disdain for makeup. She dressed professionally enough, but her trim suit made her look like a teenager playing dress-up in her mother's clothes. And being a tall girl, she wore a utilitarian pair of flats that seemed to symbolize her obvious discomfort with her own gangly body.

But the bright green eyes staring back at him through a pair of wire-rimmed glasses were as sharp as diamonds.

"Do tell me what you've discovered, Hopkins," he prodded when she didn't continue right away.

"Well, there was a query of sorts. In the system. It's complicated." She waved her hand as if the hows and whys weren't important. Crandall supposed they weren't, as long as she could tell him what those complicated things meant.

"Was it an intrusion or not?"

"I think it was."

"Can you tell where it came from?"

"That's the strange thing. It was pretty well masked, as if whoever was poking around in the system knew how to cover her tracks."

"Her tracks?"

"Or his. It's just—before the intruder could duck back into his or her shell, I discovered how they entered the system." She leaned toward him, lowering her voice. Her eyes were wide and troubled. "I think—I'm sure the intruder got in using the log-on and password of Michelle Matsumara."

Crandall went very still for a moment, trying not to react. Then he realized that he should be reacting. It was surely what the woman would expect of him upon hearing that a dead FBI employee's computer log-on had been utilized two days after her murder.

"Is there any way to track the intrusion back to the intruder?" he asked, wishing he'd been less cavalier about upgrading his rudimentary computer skills. He'd figured he'd reached a level at the FBI where understanding advanced technology could be safely left to underlings. It was his job to put the connections together, not root out the connections in the first place.

He made a note to talk to some of his associates about remedying the gaps in his technological education. Computers were clearly here to stay, and, as he had no intentions of retiring to his Virginia farm anytime soon, it would behoove him to update his skills.

Especially if he wanted to maintain absolute secrecy.

He looked across the desk at Jessica Hopkins and realized a time might come, not too distant from this moment, when he would have to have her dispatched. He hoped that time would never come. He hoped she didn't ask the wrong questions—or, he supposed, the right ones.

He wasn't one of those people who lusted for power for its own sake. He took no pleasure in some of the things he had to do in order to achieve his goals.

But he'd come to the conclusion long ago that the nation he'd pledged his life to protect was incapable of freely governing itself. Sooner or later, without the intervention of practical men such as himself, the nation would collapse beneath the weight of its own excesses.

Sadly, a country's salvation made for some very strange bedfellows indeed.

He dismissed Hopkins, asked her to keep him apprised of anything else she discovered and walked with her as far as the elevators. But once she entered and the doors swished shut behind her, he continued on to the stairs.

The walk from the J. Edgar Hoover FBI Building to the Federal Triangle Metro station took him past grand alabaster buildings that never let a person forget he was in the grandest city in the grandest nation in the world.

At least, that was the story told by the grandeur of those facades. The reality, as always in this mercurial universe, was far more debatable.

The Metro Silver Line took him to a small café in Arlington, where he sat at the counter and ordered black coffee and an apple crisp. His order arrived promptly, delivered by a quiet, clean-shaven young man who poured coffee with a smile. His dark eyes settled on Crandall's face for a moment. "Haven't seen you in here in a while."

"Haven't had occasion to be in this part of town," Crandall answered with a brief smile. He pulled his wallet from his jacket pocket and handed the server a twenty, folded around a note he'd composed on the train. "I hope to be back soon."

"I'll have your coffee and apple crisp waiting, sir." The young man took the money with a smile and carried it to the cash register. He opened the register drawer, unfolded the bill and laid it in the tray with one hand, while he pocketed the note with his other.

He nodded at Crandall and disappeared into the back of the diner.

Crandall relaxed against the stool back, enjoying a sip of the hot, strong coffee. He might lack the knowledge to make sense of what Jessica Hopkins had told him earlier in his office, but he knew plenty of people who could.

All he had to do was wait.

WHEN NICKI WAS a little girl and her world had been as changeable as the Tennessee weather, she'd found solace in cooking. It wasn't the food itself that gave her a sense of normalcy, although she'd enjoyed the results of her culinary efforts as much as anyone. It was the act of cooking, the alchemical magic of food meeting flame, that had given her a sense of calm purpose when the world around her went insane.

Her mother's emotional ups and downs had made life unpredictable, but as long as she had a stove and a pan, Nicki could control at least one part of her world. She'd taught herself to cook using an old, tattered cookbook that had belonged to her grandmother, sometimes with wretched results. But kitchen disasters had become fewer and farther between by the time she reached her teens, and her first real job in high school had been tending the grill at Maisey Ledbetter's diner. That's where she'd learned that cooking wasn't a skill but an art.

Funny how her life always seemed to cycle back to cooking, sooner or later.

Tonight, her pans were providing her a much needed distraction from Dallas's focus on his keyboard and the mysteries of the internet. She hadn't tried whipping up anything ambitious since taking up residence in this tiny little mountain town, but she'd found some nice fillets of trout at the grocery store in Abington a couple of weeks ago and had been waiting for an occasion to take them out of the freezer and do something interesting with them.

She whipped up a lemon butter sauce for the trout and tossed some fresh mixed greens and spinach into a side salad, humming tunelessly as she worked. The day's tension seemed to melt away as quickly as the butter she used in the sauce, and by the time Dallas wandered into the kitchen, sniffing the air, she was feeling relaxed and nearly optimistic again, despite the stressful news that had marred their day.

"What on earth is that amazing smell?" he murmured, bending close to look over her shoulder at the trout fillets browning on the stove.

"Trout with lemon butter sauce and a side of mixed greens in a honey vinaigrette." She struggled against the urge to lean back into his body, to wrap herself in the heat of him, though she found it harder and harder to come up with a good reason why she shouldn't.

She'd been alone for a while now. By choice.

So what if she chose something else now? Whatever was happening with Dallas Cole didn't feel rushed or reckless, despite their short time together. In some ways, she felt as if she knew him better than anyone she'd ever known.

And perhaps more to the point, she felt as if she'd shared more of herself—her true self—with him than she'd ever shared with anyone else.

She'd let him see who she was and he hadn't run away as fast as he could.

Of course, he wasn't exactly in any position to run away, was he?

"I think you're about to burn the trout," he murmured in her ear.

She removed the pan from the heat. "Sorry. I'm not used to distractions in the kitchen."

He brushed his hand down her cheek, making her shiver. "Am I a distraction?"

She turned to face him, pressing her hand flat against his chest. "By now, you have to know you are."

He gazed at her for a breathless moment. Then he bent to kiss her.

Heart pounding, she met him halfway.

Chapter Thirteen

Dallas fought the urge to scoop her up and carry her straight back to the bedroom, though the temptation was almost beyond his ability to resist. She was warm and soft, the scent of her a heady combination of sweet and tangy, stoking a level of sexual hunger he hadn't felt in ages.

And maybe if sex was all he wanted from her, he wouldn't have tried to slow things down.

But he needed more than just two bodies coming together to scratch an itch. She was his lifeline, and he had a feeling that, in a lot of ways, he was hers. That level of trust, of need, was a fragile thing.

He couldn't break it, no matter how much he wanted her.

Still, the urge to kiss her was beyond his ability to resist, especially when she rose to her toes and wrapped her arms around his neck, drawing him down to her. Her lips glided against his, lightly at first, nipping and teasing him until his head began to spin.

Then she ran the tip of her tongue against the seam of his lips, urging them apart. He deepened the kiss, relishing the sweet heat of her tongue against his, the intimacy of her hands exploring the contours of his chest.

Only when she dipped her hands under the hem of his shirt and started to push it upward did he catch her hands and hold her away from him, taking a few deep, harsh breaths to get himself back under control.

She gazed at him with desire-drunk eyes. "You're not like any man I've ever tried to seduce, Dallas Cole."

"Is that good or bad?" he asked.

She cocked her head, a smile flirting with her kiss-stung lips. "Both."

"In case it's not clear, I do want you."

She stepped closer until the soft curve of her belly pressed against his sex. "I know."

She was damn near impossible to resist, but he made himself ease her away. "We have to trust each other."

"Yes," she agreed.

"And sex complicates things."

She nodded. "It does."

"I've just found out someone I've worked with for years is dead, and it might be connected to the trouble I've gotten myself into." He took another step back, turning away from her soft gaze before he lost sight of his good sense. "It would be easy to let myself get caught up in you, as a way of forgetting my grief for my friend."

"Comfort sex."

"Yes." He stole a look at her. "I don't want there to be any doubts between us. I don't want you to ever feel used."

"A little late for that," she said in a wry tone, and he realized she was revealing more about her past than perhaps she meant to.

"I don't want you to feel used by me," he clarified firmly.

An odd light shone in her eyes. "I wouldn't. But I get it."

"And I'm not saying no forever."

"Good." Smiling, she crossed back to the stove and picked up a slotted spatula. "You still up for dinner?"

"Yeah." He smiled back at her. "Can I do anything to help?"

"There are glasses over the sink and a pitcher of iced tea in the fridge." She gave an apologetic shrug. "I don't keep wine or beer in the house. Alcoholism runs in the family, so I've learned to just steer clear."

"Tea is great. Sweet, I hope?"

She shot him a look. "Is there any other kind?"

He found the glasses and filled them with ice from the freezer before pouring the tea. "Lemon?"

"Please." She pointed to the half a lemon lying on the cutting board near the stove.

He sliced the lemon into wedges and added one to each of their drinks. By the time he found the flatware drawer, she'd plated up the trout fillets and the green salad and placed them on the table.

They ate for a few minutes in comfortable silence. The trout was delicious, cooked to a delicate flakiness that rivaled anything Dallas had eaten in any of the fancier restaurants in Washington. "How long have you been cooking?" he asked a few minutes later.

"Since I was a kid." A smile played at her lips. "When I was younger, my life was pure chaos. I had to fend for myself a lot, and cooking was something I could control. If we had food in the house, I could make my own meal. I found comfort in being able to feed myself that way. It made me feel less vulnerable, not having to depend on my mother to put food on the table. Because when she was drunk or high, she'd forget to eat for days at a time, and she certainly wasn't thinking about me."

"I'm sorry."

"It's not a good life for a kid, but it made me

tough. I don't regret those life lessons. I've survived because of them."

He reached across the table. "Survival isn't enough."

"Sometimes it has to be."

"I want more than survival." He held on to her hand, brushed his thumb across her knuckles. "I want more for you."

When she looked up at him, her eyes were damp. "Thank you."

He knew he should stop while he was ahead, but the anxiety eating away at his insides wouldn't allow him to remain silent. "Nicki, I know you've worked hard to get in a position to go inside the BRI. But what you're about to do could get you killed."

She dropped her fork and put her other hand over his. "Walking out the door can get you killed. Pulling your car onto the road can get you killed."

"Don't be flippant."

"I'm not. I'm just being realistic. Life is a risk. All of it. I could play it safe and still die in a senseless accident on any given day. Then what good would my life have been?"

"So this is your way of living a life of meaning?"

"I guess it is."

He wanted to argue, but he understood her feelings. One of the reasons he'd decided to train for a position in the FBI's cybersecurity division was to do something more significant with his life than putting together recruiting packets and public relations pamphlets.

"I'm going into this with my eyes wide-open," she said when he didn't respond. "I am. I know the danger I'm getting into. But I'm the right person to do this job. You know I am."

As much as he'd like to deny it, she was right. She'd managed to put herself in the right place at the right time to get closer to the top of the Blue Ridge Infantry than anyone had managed before. "How did you manage it? How did Quinn know you'd be the right person?"

"I don't know," she admitted. "I think it helps that I come from the hills, just like they do. I know what life here can be like, and I understand the struggles and frustrations that make them feel so powerless that they think the only way to control their lives is to take drastic steps like joining a militia. I get them, way more than I like to admit." Her voice lowered to a raspy half whisper. "I *was* them, in a lot of ways for a lot of years."

He'd gotten out of Harlan County young enough to escape the worst of that sort of desperation, in large part thanks to a high school teacher who'd seen his potential. He knew he was very fortunate.

It hurt to think of Nicki having to fight her way

out of the poverty and desperation on her own, but it was a powerful testament to her inner decency that she'd managed to find her way back to a sense of purpose.

Even if that purpose was about to put her life in grave danger.

"Did you leave a message for Quinn about your breakthrough?" He poked at the remainder of his trout, his appetite long gone.

"Yes. I'm hoping he'll be able to get a message back to me before my meeting tomorrow." She nodded at his food. "You don't like it?"

"It's delicious. I'm just not as hungry as I thought."

She smiled, her expression sympathetic. "Worried about me?"

"Yeah. Is that allowed?"

"It's appreciated." She reached across the table and brushed her fingers over his. "Want to get out of here later tonight?"

He arched an eyebrow. "Out in the open?"

"Up the mountain." She nodded her head toward the hill rising behind the cabin. "I thought I'd check the drop site before bedtime. I know it might be too early, but I can use the exercise. How about you?"

He realized what she was offering, the level of trust in him to which she was admitting. "You're going to let me see your dead drop?"

"This is about your life now, as much as it's about mine." She drew her hand back and rose, picking up her plate. "I'll put the leftovers up so you'll have something to eat tomorrow while I'm at my meeting."

He followed her with his own plate. "Do you think they'll want you to go right away? If you end up getting hired to be this guy's caretaker."

"I'd have to come back and pack."

He felt a flicker of relief. He'd get one more chance to talk her out of it, then. Not that he thought he'd be successful.

She was a headstrong woman. It was one of her charms.

"How's the computer magic coming?" she asked as she put the leftover food into containers for the refrigerator.

"Slowly," he admitted. "I'm trying not to leave any traces of my intrusions."

"Have you been successful?"

"I don't know. I think so, mostly. It's not really possible to intrude on a secure network without leaving some traces, but you try to leave them in places where most people wouldn't think to look. And it's not like the networks I'm looking through are going to be monitored carefully for a breach in the areas I'm targeting."

"What if they are?"

"They'll still have to be smart and lucky to catch it."

He didn't tell her where he was looking for clues. Breaching the FBI's network was dangerous as hell, and she'd probably be about as happy about the risks he was taking as he was about her meeting tomorrow with Del McClintock and his boss.

But he needed to know Crandall's secret connections. He needed a way to prove the AD was crooked if he was ever going to be able to clear his good name. If it meant taking big risks, well, Nicki wasn't the only person who was willing to put her neck on the line for a life of meaning.

JOHN BARTHOLOMEW HAD lived in a modest but comfortable apartment in Abingdon, Virginia, for the past few months while he worked as a security consultant by day and glorified errand boy by night. The money wasn't great, but if he wanted a job that paid well, he'd have stuck to accounting.

He'd wanted a job that had meaning. The kind of job he'd had once, the kind of job he'd been forced to leave behind.

He'd been a good spy, while it lasted. He had the sort of face people didn't seem to remember once he'd passed from their field of sight. Average height, average build, hair that was neither black nor blond but somewhere in between, darker in the winter and lighter in the summer. He was neither fair-skinned nor olive-skinned, his eyes neither blue nor brown but a sort of murky hazel that shifted with his mood.

If he had possessed a criminal bent, he probably could have gotten away with any number of crimes, because nobody would have remembered what he looked like when all was said and done.

Only his speech drew people's attention, the mountain twang of his eastern Tennessee roots he'd never quite been able to lose. Here in the foothills of the Blue Ridge Mountains, he fit in almost like a native. Being nondescript was an asset in his business.

Nobody seemed to notice when he left his apartment shortly after sunset and drove to a scenic overlook on Bellwether Road, where he left his truck and started hiking up the mountainside to the drop site.

He left the note from Alexander Quinn with a minimum of fuss before hurrying down the mountain as quickly as he'd climbed it. On his way back to Abingdon, he stopped at a convenience store for a six-pack of beer and was back in his apartment, sock-clad feet propped on his coffee table, before nine o'clock. If anyone had noticed him leave or arrive, they weren't likely to be curious about it. Who didn't go for a beer run now and then?

Window shades down, TV turned up, he pulled the note Nicki had left him earlier that day from his pocket and read the scrawled message again.

She had finally set up a meeting with their mark, which meant that the scrappy girl from Ridge County, Tennessee, had managed to disarm the notoriously suspicious Blue Ridge Infantry crew where dozens of men before her had failed.

Or had she? Was her planned meeting with Del McClintock and his mysterious boss really just another test of her trustworthiness?

The most dangerous test of all?

She would check the drop site before tomorrow, which meant she'd find Alexander Quinn's instructions before her meeting. Like Agent X, Quinn seemed wary of trusting this stroke of fortune, as well.

He opened one of the beers and took a sip, reminding himself there was only so much of this operation that he could control. It was a fact that he sometimes found very hard to take. For a man who craved action, who longed for an occupation with real meaning, the hardest part of his job was what he was currently doing.

Sitting and waiting.

THE NIGHT AIR was cold and sharp, but it felt ridiculously good as it filled Dallas's lungs. The trek up the mountain left him winded and tired, but he made it without collapsing, something he wouldn't have been able to accomplish only a few days earlier. The physical remnants of his ordeal with the Blue Ridge Infantry had mostly faded from his body over the past few days. Only the psychic scars remained.

Those, he suspected, might take a while to disappear.

But reaching the small cave near the top of the mountain ridge felt like a victory, so he enjoyed it as well as he could while gasping for breath.

"You still hanging in there?" Nicki asked as he leaned against the cold stone wall of the cave's exterior.

He nodded, too winded to reply.

She brushed her hand down his arm as she passed him and entered the dark cave, disappearing from his sight. She emerged a moment later and nodded at him. "You need to rest a little longer?"

He wanted to say no, but the truth was, he needed to sit for a moment, let his flagging body catch up with his stubborn will. He nodded at the fallen log nearby, which she'd turned onto its side before entering the cave. "I take it that log means something?"

"It's our signal. He turns it up. I turn it down. Sit there if you need to."

He sat on the fallen tree trunk. "Did you read the note?"

Nodding, she sat next to him, keeping her voice low. "Quinn is worried this might be another test. He said I shouldn't assume I'm in yet."

"He's right."

"I know." She scooted over until their bodies touched, leaning her head against his shoulder. He put his arm around her, keeping her close.

"It's not too late to back out if you want to."

She sighed, her breath condensing in the cold night air, rising in whorls of vapor. "I can't back out. Not when we're so close."

"What if he wants you to move in with him?"

"I'm assuming that's exactly what he'll want." She sat up, looking at him. "It's what we want, too. To get that close, to be right there on the inside, gathering information—it's why I came here."

"How am I going to know if you're okay?"

"You won't. Not right away." She took his hand and held it. Her fingers were cold but the warmth of her enveloped him, anyway, driving away the chill of the night. "Maybe we should arrange for Quinn to extract you. He can put you in one of our safe houses in Tennessee."

"I don't know Quinn. I don't trust him." He met her gaze, his heart throbbing heavily in his chest. "I trust you."

"Then stay in my cabin, the way we planned." She rose to her feet, tugging him up from the log. "Ready to go home?"

Home, he thought bleakly as he fell in step with her as they headed back down the mountain.

The cabin wouldn't feel like home once she was gone.

THE KNOCK ON the front door came late in the evening, as Philip Crandall was preparing for bed. His wife, Melinda, preferred life on their horse farm in Fairfax County, so he kept an apartment in the city during the week and commuted on weekends.

He rarely had visitors at the apartment, and never from people at the Bureau, which meant one of two things. Either the person at his door had the wrong apartment—or his trip to the diner in Arlington had produced results sooner than he'd anticipated.

When he opened the door to a young man dressed in a bright red polo shirt emblazoned with a pizza chain logo, he first assumed it was the former, a pizza delivery to the wrong apartment.

But when he looked into the familiar blue eyes of the diner barista who'd taken his note with the twenty that afternoon, he realized his error.

"Pizza delivery," the young man said. "That'll be fifteen dollars."

"I only have a twenty," Crandall said.

The young man smiled. "I can make change."

Crandall pulled out his wallet and handed over the twenty. The man returned a folded five to him and gave him the pizza box. "Enjoy, sir."

Crandall closed the door and locked it, then carried the pizza box to the coffee table. He sat and looked at the closed pizza box, his heart suddenly pounding.

Surely the man wouldn't have come all the way out here if the news wasn't significant. Would he?

Remembering the way he'd delivered his request earlier that day at the diner, Crandall unfolded the five-dollar bill. Inside, he found a small square of paper with four words written on it: *check under the pizza.*

He stared down at the pizza box, suddenly tense. He hadn't yet experienced any difficulties in dealing with the men he had chosen to be his unlikely comrades, but he'd always known that aligning himself with them held inherent risks. There could come a time, at any moment, when they decided he was no longer of any use to them.

And it would be so very easy to dispatch him with a simple shrapnel bomb hidden inside a pizza box, would it not?

"Life is a gamble, Phil." His father's gravelly

voice rang in his head. *"You can't win if you don't play, so suck it up and roll the dice."*

Crandall took a deep breath and opened the pizza box.

Nothing exploded. The contents were just eight slices of pepperoni and mushroom pizza. He released a gusty sigh and picked up one of the pieces to look beneath it.

There was a clear plastic bag lying flat beneath the pizza. He tugged it free, wiped off the dusting of semolina flour and looked at the note inside.

"We've tracked the intrusion to a cell phone signal bouncing off a tower in Dudley County, Virginia," the note said. Beneath that terse announcement were several details, including the coordinates of the cell tower in question.

Dudley County, Virginia, Crandall thought. *Why does that sound familiar?*

He dug in his pocket for the burner phone he used for his more secretive pursuits and dialed a number. The person on the other end of the line answered on the second ring. "What do you want?"

"Information," he answered. Then he outlined what he needed to know. "By morning?"

"It'll cost you."

"It always does." He hung up the phone and reached for the slice of pizza he'd moved aside, suddenly starving.

Chapter Fourteen

Friday turned out to be a beautiful day, sunny and mild. Nicki wanted to believe the fine weather was a good omen, that her meeting this afternoon would go well and she'd finally get this undercover operation running on all cylinders.

There was just one problem. She didn't believe in good omens. And once this operation really got underway, she'd be in the gravest danger of her life, far away from anyone who gave a damn about her or her safety.

"You don't have to go through with this." Dallas's voice was a warm rumble behind her. The heat of his body washed over hers as he crossed to stand behind her at the kitchen window.

"Yes, I do." Of its own volition, her body swayed backward until she rested against his chest.

He wrapped his arms around her waist, holding her loosely. "No, you don't. Quinn shouldn't have put you in this position to begin with. You're not a trained agent, are you?"

"I've had experience working with agencies—"

"As an informant, not an undercover operative."

"I'd be essentially an informant in this situation, too. Besides, I was sort of undercover at the farm." Although, given how badly things had ended for Jeff Burwell, maybe that wasn't such a good example to bring up.

Dallas felt so solid behind her, so steady, she wished there was a way she could take him with her, stash him away in her luggage so that when she was alone and scared on this upcoming mission, she could pull him out, wrap his arms around her like a warm sweater and feel this safe again.

"It's not the same thing." He tightened his hold on her, pressing his cheek against her temple. The rough bristles of his morning beard pricked her skin, sending a light shiver down her spine.

"I've got three more hours before I have to go meet Del. Can't we talk about something else?" She turned in his arms to face him, flattening her hands against his chest. "Tell me something I don't know about you."

His lips curved in a brief smile. "This game will bore you to death."

"I'll be the judge of that." She tugged the lapel

of his shirt. "I never did find you that desk. I need to do that before I leave for my new job."

"What if he wants you to leave right away?"

"I'll tell him I need to give notice at work and talk to my landlord. They can't expect me to drop everything and go to work today." She shook her head. "If I agreed to that, I'd come across as entirely too eager. I'll make them meet some of my terms before I'll meet some of theirs."

He tugged her closer. "You're a tough negotiator, huh?"

"I can be."

"Good to know."

She moved closer to him, pressing her cheek against his collarbone. "I wish I had a way to stay in touch with you while I'm gone."

"How are you going to stay in touch with Quinn?"

"There's a tracking device on my key chain. Quinn can find me wherever I am." She could tell by the sudden tension in Dallas's body that he didn't like the sound of that solution. "I have to trust Quinn. He's taken care of me this far."

"Do you know the coordinates of your tracker? For today? I could track you myself—"

She drew back to look at him. "I told you, this is just a meeting. I'm not going anywhere yet."

His brow creased. "It would make me feel better if I could keep an eye on you." He flashed a quick, sheepish smile. "That sounds kind of pathetic, doesn't it?"

"It sounds really sweet, actually." She rose to press her lips against his. With effort, she kept the kiss light, even though the need to draw him even closer, kiss him even more deeply, welled inside her like floodwaters seeking to breach a weakening dam.

He threaded his fingers through her hair, holding her still while he returned her kiss with more desperation, crumbling her defenses until she wrapped herself around him, drinking in every bit of passion he offered.

The sound of a phone ringing down the hall made her groan. Dallas released a deep sigh against her lips. "That's going to be Del, isn't it?"

She nodded.

"Don't answer," he whispered, bending to kiss her again.

The temptation to give in was nearly overwhelming, but she pulled free of his grasp and went down the hall to answer the phone on her bedside table. "Hello?"

"Hey there, Nicki. Just wanted to make sure you were up and getting ready for our meeting today."

"Of course. I'm looking forward to it." She sat on the bed and looked up as Dallas came to stand in the doorway, watching her. "Is there anything I need to know before the meeting?"

"I've talked you up to him, so I think he really just wants to talk to you about what your duties would be. He wants to get his health back under control without having to deal with doctors and hospitals."

"He's going to have to have a doctor to prescribe medication," she warned. "There's a limit to what I can do for him."

"He knows that. Trust me, sugar. He's going to love you."

Maybe it was a case of the nerves, but something about Del's cheerful tone was starting to make her second-guess her decision to let him drive her to the meeting. "Listen, I know we planned to meet at the diner so you could drive me to the meeting, but can't I just meet you wherever your friend is going to be? If I'm going to work with him, I'm going to need to know how to get there, anyway, right?"

There was a taut pause on the other end of the line. "All in good time," he said finally, his tone a little sharper than it had been before. "He's been clear about how he wants this to take place, and I don't think we should make him feel uncomfortable right out of the gate, do you?"

"Of course not," she said quickly, not wanting

to give him any reason to back out. "I'll meet you at the diner as planned."

"You'll knock his socks off," Del said. "Trust me."

"I do," she lied. "Thank you so much for setting this up. I'll see you around eleven?"

"See you then, sugar. Bye now."

She hung up the phone and looked at Dallas. "Am I crazy to do this?"

"Yes," he answered flatly.

"I can't back out now."

His jaw tightened and his eyes flashed with anger as he gazed back at her, but he didn't speak. He didn't have to. He'd already told her his opinion of the job Quinn was asking her to do. But she was too close to her goal to stop now.

She had to see it through.

Starting with today's meeting.

TECHNICALLY, JOHN BARTHOLOMEW didn't work for Alexander Quinn. Instead, he worked for a limited liability corporation called Citadel Properties, a security consulting firm with which Quinn had signed a contract. But the truth was, Citadel had only one employee. And Quinn kept that one employee pretty damned busy.

On the desk beside him sat a folder containing several job applications Quinn had faxed over earlier in the week. After experiencing some troubling issues with his in-house vetting procedures the previous year, Quinn had decided to contract out the background checks for his company.

Before the end of the week, John would have to make his way through those resumes and make sure that Quinn didn't make any hiring decisions that would come back to bite him.

But first, he had a meeting to attend.

The drive from Abingdon to River's End took almost thirty minutes, most of that time spent on winding two-lane roads that wound around the mountains and dipped into shady hollows deep in the backwoods of the Blue Ridge Mountains.

Dugan's Diner wasn't much to look at from the outside, just a boxy glass-front eatery on the main road into town. At a quarter to eleven, the parking lot was just starting to fill up for the midday crowd. John parked to one side, near the road, to give him a decent view of any cars entering or exiting the area.

Quinn hadn't told him specifically to tail Nicki and Del McClintock to the secondary meeting place, but he hadn't told him not to, either. John was still considering his options when he saw Nicki's Jeep pull into the lot and park a row away from the front.

He picked up the small pair of binoculars lying on the seat beside him and took a quick look at her through the driver's side window. She looked tense. Understandable. He was tense on her behalf. But he hoped she'd get her nerves under control before McClintock arrived. The success of this operation might well depend on her being able to keep a cool head.

His cell phone trilled in his pocket, giving him a start. He checked the display and found the number was blocked.

Quinn, of course. His boss didn't bother with the niceties. "You have her in sight?"

John lowered his binoculars. "I do."

"Don't interfere. I don't know how well trained McClintock might be, but you can't risk his catching you tailing him."

John swallowed a sigh.

"Are we clear?" Quinn asked, steel in his voice.

"Perfectly."

"Is the tracker working?"

John picked up the tablet lying on the passenger seat and brushed his fingertip across the screen. The GPS tracking software popped into view, a flashing green light indicating Nicki Jamison's current position on the map. "Working fine."

"Let's hope she keeps that key chain on her at all times."

John spotted a blue Chevy Silverado pulling into the parking lot. It stopped behind Nicki's Jeep, engine revving.

"McClintock's here," John told Quinn.

"Is he alone?"

"Seems to be." He lifted the binoculars and took a good look at the truck. McClintock sat alone in the cab. "Just him."

As he watched, Nicki exited the Jeep and walked toward the passenger door of the Silverado. She opened the door and climbed into the cab, gracing McClintock with a nervous smile.

The door closed and the Silverado pulled out of the parking lot into the light stream of traffic on the main road. They disappeared around the curve.

"She's gone off with McClintock," he told Quinn.

"Tracker still working?"

John checked the GPS tracker. On the move with the truck. "Yes."

"Keep an eye on the tracker. I'll be in touch." Quinn hung up.

John put his phone in his pocket and cranked his engine. The urge to ignore Quinn's orders and follow the Silverado set John's nerves on edge, but he forced himself to turn the wheel and head down the highway in the opposite direction. Nicki Jamison was a resourceful woman who'd smashed through barriers to the Blue Ridge Infantry's inner circle that experienced agents hadn't been able to get beyond.

He had to trust her to do her job, just like he had to do his.

He had almost reached the road back to Abingdon when his phone rang again. He pushed the speaker button and answered. "Yeah?"

It was Quinn. "We have a situation."

THERE WAS NO KNOCK, just the rattle of keys in the door and the creak as it opened. Dallas quickly closed the laptop and picked up the baseball bat Nicki had given him that morning before she left for the diner.

Pushing to his feet, he headed for the door to the makeshift office, easing a quick look down the hallway. His heart skipped a beat as a man stepped into the hall, his gaze locking with Dallas's.

"Get out of here or I'll call the cops," Dallas growled, pulling himself up to his full height and swinging the bat in front of him.

The other man's eyebrows rose, but he didn't look overly worried. "You're not going to call the cops, Mr. Cole, because they're already looking for you." He held up his hands, showing they were empty. Dallas didn't see any sign of a weapon on him. "My name is John Bartholomew. I work with Alexander Quinn. I've got to get you out of here."

Dallas tightened his grip on the bat, caught off

guard by the man's terse announcement. "Alexander who?"

"Don't insult my intelligence, Cole. I'm the man who picked up Nicki's messages on the mountain, including the information about your unexpected intrusion into her undercover operation. She calls me Agent X."

How would he know what Nicki called her contact? Unless—

No. Maybe this man had intercepted something. Or worse—what if he'd gotten his hands on Nicki herself?

"I'm who I say I am," the man who'd introduced himself as John Bartholomew said brusquely. "But I don't have time to prove that to your satisfaction. So I really, really need you to take a leap of faith here."

"Why don't you have time?" Dallas asked, his grip on the bat so tight that his fingers had begun to feel numb from the pressure.

"Because there are FBI agents heading this way right now, with plans to take you into custody. They could arrive at any moment, so it would be in your best interests to get the hell out of here while we still can."

"And I'm supposed to take your word for it?"

The other man sighed deeply, as if he was growing exasperated with Dallas's stalling. "How about Cade Landry's word?" He lowered one of his hands and reached for his pocket.

Dallas took an instinctive step back toward the storage room, putting the door frame between him and the other man. "Put your hands back up."

The man withdrew his hand from his pocket, a cell phone clutched between his fingers and thumb. "Quinn texted me a video link. He thought you might need persuasion." He turned the phone toward Dallas. "You'll need to come closer."

Dallas shook his head. "Put the phone on the floor and slide it to me."

One of the man's eyebrows lifted, but he did as Dallas said. Dallas stopped the sliding phone with his foot.

"Turn your back and put your hands up on the walls."

John turned around and lifted his hands, pressing his palms flat against the walls on either side of him.

Dallas crouched and picked up the phone, keeping his eyes on John until he had the phone in his hand. He glanced at the screen. There was a video link cued up. Pressing his lips to a thin line, he hit the play button.

A familiar face filled the screen. "Cole, it's Landry. Quinn seems to think you're going to be your typical pain-in-the-ass self, so listen quick.

John Bartholomew is telling you the truth. Get out of the cabin now."

"How do I know this wasn't filmed under duress?" Dallas asked aloud.

"By the way, nobody's forcing me to record this," Landry continued on the video, as if anticipating his question. The man actually smiled a little, as if he knew he'd predicted Dallas's reaction correctly. "Olivia says hello. Now please get the hell out of there."

The video ended, and Dallas looked up at John. Before he could speak, John's cell phone rang, nearly scaring Dallas out of his skin.

John looked at Dallas over his shoulder. "That's Quinn. He's the only person who has that number. I need to answer it. He may have new information."

Dallas pushed the Talk button. "Quinn?"

There was a pause on the other end of the line before the man spoke. "Dallas Cole, I presume?"

"Why did you send your errand boy to come get me?"

"He didn't tell you?"

"I'd like to hear it from you," Dallas said tightly.

"There's no time." Quinn sounded impatient.

"Make time."

"I have contacts in the FBI who informed me that certain intrusions into their computer system have led them to believe you are trying to hack the FBI's network." Dallas could hear the irritation in Quinn's voice over the phone. "They've somehow traced the intrusion to a system working off a cell phone operating in Dudley County, Virginia. They're sending agents from the Bristol resident agency. They should be there within the next twenty minutes. I suggest you get out now."

Dallas glared at John, who was watching him with wary eyes.

Quinn's voice sharpened. "By the way, once you leave, I suggest you ask John to show you the GPS system he has tracking Nicki's whereabouts."

John spoke up, his expression alarmed. "Why's that?"

"Because," Quinn answered in a voice as sharp as shattered glass, "the Blue Ridge Infantry has somehow figured out Nicki is an undercover operative."

Chapter Fifteen

The radio in Del's Silverado was cranked up high, tuned to a satellite station playing headbanging metal so loudly that Nicki couldn't think. She stole a look at Del, who was drumming the frenetic bass line on the steering wheel as he drove about twenty miles an hour over the speed limit.

She supposed once a man decided to get involved with domestic terrorism, speed laws posed no particular impediment to his whims.

"How much farther?" she asked, having to raise her voice over the radio. They'd been driving for nearly twenty minutes, moving deeper into the mountains as they left River's End behind. She hadn't ventured this far into the mountains in her time in River's End, so she wasn't really sure exactly where they were going.

"Not far," he answered, flashing her a smile that made the skin on the back of her neck prickle.

Something wasn't right. She couldn't point to any one thing that raised her suspicions, but all of her instincts were telling her that she needed to proceed with extreme caution.

She couldn't demand that Del turn the truck around and head back to River's End, not without throwing away everything she'd worked for. But she intended to move forward on high alert. The first minute anything started to go sideways, she had to have a plan of escape.

She wasn't armed. She'd grown up with an aversion to firearms, given her mother's steady stream of well-armed boyfriends who thought nothing of scaring the hell out of a little girl who got in their way. Alexander Quinn had insisted on training her how to use a weapon in case she ever had to, but she always hoped like hell she'd never have to.

She was beginning to rethink her position on guns, however, the deeper into the woods Del drove her.

"Is this where your friend lives?" she asked, peering through the windshield at the thickening woods. In this part of the mountains, what houses and buildings existed sparsely dotted a landscape of untamed acres of dense woodlands where evergreens outnumbered hardwoods.

It would be easy to get lost in these woods, she thought, her skin prickling madly. Lost and gone forever.

A dirt road crossed the road ahead, and finally

the Silverado slowed, preparing to turn. Nicki eyed the narrow dirt road with apprehension. Just how far back in the woods did Del's boss live?

Once on the dirt road, Del was forced to drive with considerably more care, the ruts and bumps putting the truck's shocks to a grueling test. The jouncing and bucking didn't do much to calm Nicki's suddenly jangling nerves, but she tried to remain steady, at least outwardly.

Del was taking her to meet the man she'd been trying to meet since she first showed up in River's End. It was happening faster than anybody had hoped. That was good news, right?

So why didn't it feel like good news?

"Almost there," Del said, his mouth curving in a broad smile.

Something about that smile set Nicki's teeth on edge. Maybe because it looked feral and hungry.

Like a predator with his eyes on the prize.

"THEY'VE STOPPED." Dallas darted a quick look at John Bartholomew. The other man drove with an enviable combination of skill and speed, eating up the distance between their location and the blinking red dot on the GPS locator map.

"Address?" John asked.

"It's not really an address. It's not even a road, as far as I can tell." Dallas peered at the tablet, trying to zoom in for a better look. "The last road they were on seems to be Partlow Road. Heading east in the general direction of Saltville."

John released a quiet sigh. "I should have anticipated this."

"Yeah," Dallas agreed in a tight growl. "You should've."

"She wanted to do this work," John added, glancing toward Dallas. "She asked Quinn for the chance. Did you know that?"

"I know she was involved in an incident where the BRI attacked someone she was working for."

"Someone she was informing on," John corrected. "Burned him out of house and home. Nearly killed his kids."

"She said that guy wasn't really involved with the BRI."

"He wasn't. But she didn't know that when she signed up to inform on him."

Dallas glared at the other man. "Your point?"

"My point is, this ain't her first rodeo." John's tone flattened into a drawl. "She knew what she agreed to when she took this job. No point in arguing about whether she should have been undercover in the first place. She chose to do it and now she's in serious trouble. Quinn can't get backup here for another few hours, so it's up to the two of us to get her out of there alive. Are you with me or not?"

"Of course, I'm with you." He turned his attention to the GPS tracking program on the tablet. "My guess is, they turned off on a drive or road that's not marked on the GPS map."

John waved his hand toward the GPS navigation system built into the dashboard of his truck. "Can you feed the last four coordinates into that?"

"Sure." Dallas entered the coordinates. "Once we get to number three, we need to start looking for a turnoff on the left."

They fell silent as the GPS intoned the directions for the first set of coordinates. After a few moments, John asked, "What sort of physical condition are you in?"

Dallas looked up, surprised. "Not top form, but I'm in a hell of a lot better shape than I was a few days ago."

"You were their captive." It wasn't a question.

"For about three weeks."

"Any idea where?"

Dallas gave it some thought. "Couldn't have been too far from here, actually. As soon as I escaped, I headed west. I ended up falling flat on my face somewhere in the mountains."

"On Bellwether Road," John murmured, his tone thoughtful.

Dallas looked down at the tablet, scanning the GPS tracker map. Looking a little closer, he located Bellwether Road.

Due west of the spot where the red dot indicated Nicki's current position.

Panic tightened his gut. "Do you think they've taken her to the place where they were holding me?"

"Not sure," John admitted. "It's just interesting. Don't you think?"

Interesting wasn't the word Dallas would have used. *Terrifying* seemed more appropriate. "We can't just drive in there, you know. If that really is the place where they were keeping me, there are armed thugs everywhere."

"We'll have to go on foot. Figure something out when we get closer and have some idea what we're up against."

As Dallas started to respond, the GPS navigation program announced their arrival at their first set of coordinates and gave directions to the next spot on the map.

"What can you remember about the place where you were held captive?" John asked.

"It's in the woods. Up in the hills. There was a cabin, but that's not where they kept me. Not far from the cabin, they had a root cellar built into the ground. They stuck me down there. They had shackles screwed into the cinder block walls. Like a damn dungeon." He shuddered at the memory. "I wonder how many men they've kept in that place over the years."

"They have other places like that," John said. "Not just here in Virginia."

"I know. Nicki told me Cade Landry spent some time chained up in a basement in some cabin down in Tennessee."

"That's what I hear," John said quietly. "Is this going to be too much for you? If we get there and it's the same place?"

It was a fair question, Dallas had to admit. Even now, his gut ached with apprehension at the thought of being back in that place. He could still feel the dank chill, the smell of mold and sweat and fear. The darkness, at times, had been a living thing, every bit as threatening as the gun-toting men with beards who'd enforced his captivity.

No, he didn't want to go back there ever again. He didn't want to relive a single one of those memories.

But if that's where they were taking Nicki, he'd do it. Because the only thing that scared him more than what he'd already been through was the thought of never seeing her again.

ONCE UPON A TIME, in what seemed a lifetime ago, Nicolette Destiny Jamison had thought the world was a place full of infinite possibilities. She'd always had a flair for the dramatic, and at the age of seven, the inescapable facts of a foolish, alcoholic mother who made bad choices and the total absence of a father in her life had seemed little more than the melodramatic trappings of her life story.

She was going to be somebody. Someone important. Someone beautiful and elegant, a secret princess who would emerge from her chrysalis— a word she'd learned that very day at school—and wow the world with her shiny, rainbow-colored wings.

Then she'd stumbled on the body in the woods. It was a man, or at least, she thought it must have been, from the grimy, tattered remains of his clothing. There were hands, bloated and discolored. Shoes that could barely contain the gas-swollen girth of his feet. And his face—what the insects and wildlife had done to his face had fueled nightmares for months.

And in those nightmares, she'd come to the grim realization that princesses didn't come from the hills and hollows of Ridge County, Tennessee. Drug addicts and alcoholics did. People who killed other people over women or money or just a bad mood and left them to rot in the woods.

Nothing she could do, or dream, or scheme, was ever going to change that fact.

Nicki Jamison had given up her dreams for a long, long time. Until she met Jeff Burwell and his three little kids.

It wasn't that she'd fallen in love with him.

She hadn't. Not in any romantic way. But in Jeff she'd found someone who'd come from the hills, just as she had. Someone who'd made the life he loved, tilling the soil, tending it with the same sort of love and patience with which he reared his three motherless children. He wasn't a storybook prince, but he was living a life of meaning and joy, even in the face of his lingering grief.

She'd started to believe again that she could have that kind of life for herself. Maybe she wouldn't be a princess with iridescent wings. Maybe she wouldn't charm a prince into undying love and devotion.

But her life could mean something. It didn't have to be an endless series of misadventures and mistakes. She could be happy if she could just find something she loved as much as Jeff loved his family and his farm.

When the Blue Ridge Infantry had burned his dream to the ground, she had taken it personally. She'd grieved his loss deeply because in a way, it had been her loss, as well.

The loss of hope for that future of happiness.

She hadn't heard from Jeff since the Tennessee Bureau of Investigation had hurried her out of Thurlow Gap, safely away from the men who'd taken their devastating revenge on the man they considered a traitor. The TBI wouldn't give her any updates, even when she'd asked. Her TBI handler, Martin, had stopped taking her calls finally, leaving an underling to tell her to stop calling and move on with her life.

She just hadn't known how to do that. Not until she'd met Alexander Quinn and talked him into giving her a job.

A purpose.

Beside her in the Silverado, Del McClintock had begun humming off-key along with the radio, but his lips were still curled in a half smile that gave her the creeps.

Wait it out, she told herself, even as she started taking furtive looks around the truck cab for something she could turn into a weapon if she started to lose control of the situation.

But the cab was clutter-free. There wasn't even an ice scraper in sight.

Through the trees ahead, she saw what looked like the corner edge of a cabin. Thirty yards later, the entire cabin came into view.

Four men stood in front of the cabin, armed with rifles. They weren't aiming at the approaching truck, at least, Nicki thought, swallowing a nervous giggle. That was a good sign, wasn't it?

"Expecting trouble?" she asked Del, turning to look at him.

Her gaze never made it to his face, locking instead on the barrel of the big black pistol he held pointed at her heart. "Sugar, you've got trouble written all over your pretty face."

"I don't understand." Nicki stared at the pistol and tried not to let her brain get too far ahead of her fear. If she was the innocent woman she was pretending to be, she'd be freaking out entirely.

Sort of exactly the way she *was* freaking out.

"Did you think we wouldn't figure it out, Nicki?" Del's predatory smile widened. "Do you think you're dealing with a bunch of stupid hicks?"

"Figure out what?" She couldn't even make a run for it, surrounded as they were by men with rifles. And it wasn't as if she could get out of the truck before Del shot her dead, anyway. He was too close to miss.

"You're working for the cops, aren't you?"

She stared at him, genuinely dumbfounded. He thought she was working for the cops? What the hell? "What are you talking about?"

"One of our guys dropped by the diner the other day during your shift. He kept thinking he recognized you, and it finally came to him. You were Nicki Geralds, the woman who worked for his cousin down in Thurlow Gap, Tennessee."

Nicki Geralds had been the pseudonym she'd used when she was working for Jeff Burwell. "Are you talking about Jeff?"

Del looked surprised. "You're admitting it?"

"I worked as a housekeeper and nanny for a guy named Jeff Burwell after his wife died. I wasn't there long—there was a fire—"

"Nicki *Geralds*?"

"My married name," she lied. "I was still using it then, even though the divorce was almost final."

For a moment, Del looked uncertain. "You were married before?"

"Yes."

"You never mentioned that."

She frowned. "It wasn't a happy marriage. He was a serial cheater. And he treated me like garbage. I don't like talking about that time in my life. It's embarrassing and painful." She frowned at the pistol still pointing at her chest. "Please put that down. You're really st-starting to scare me."

He didn't lower the pistol, but he shifted it to his left, the barrel now pointing toward the dashboard instead. "Darby said the boys in Tennessee were all sure you were just playing Jeff. Trying to get him to turn his back on his kin and inform on them to the FBI."

She tried not to react, but this was the first she'd heard that anyone had even suspected her time with Jeff Burwell had been anything but aboveboard. "That's crazy. My God, Del, the FBI? Do you know what kind of thugs work for the FBI? We've talked about this, haven't we?"

"Was it just talk?" His look of uncertainty

shifted to suspicion, and she realized she was starting to lose him again. "What did you and your FBI buddies do, profile me? One of those militia nuts, right? Bitch about the government, flash him a pretty smile, wear a tight-cut blouse and painted-on jeans, and the stupid backwoods hick'll buy anything you're tryin' to sell." His voice rose to a roar. "Right?"

The pistol barrel whipped back toward her heart.

"No! God, Del!" She shrank back, not pretending the rush of paralyzing fear. He was furious with her now. His rage blazed in his eyes, reminding her of the inferno that had whipped across the fields that night in Thurlow Gap, whipped by the night wind. It had spread wildly, eating up everything in its path.

The door behind her opened, and she would have tumbled out if not for the seat belt holding her in place. A pair of arms caught her as her torso pitched backward when the door behind her back fell away.

Del's eyes widened, and he lowered the pistol.

Whoever held her from behind smelled like… bacon and toast.

She pulled away from the arms grasping her and turned to see who had caught her.

Trevor Colley stood in the open door, a faint smile curving his lips. "Surprised to see me?"

She stared at him, her mind reeling. What was the diner manager doing out here in the middle of this mess? "I don't understand."

He shook his head. "Your problem, Nicki, is that you think you know how to read people. You're not bad at it, really. I mean, you read Del here in a heartbeat. Saw he was the one you'd have to deal with if you wanted to get anywhere around these parts, right? 'Cause he's a little bit smarter, a little more powerful than the others. A born leader, right?"

Her pulse thundered in her head as she stared at the man she'd worked with for months now without ever suspecting a thing. "You hate the BRI."

"Do I?" His smile widened. "Or is that just what I wanted you to believe?"

"Why?" she asked. "Were you trying to set me up or something? Why would you do that? What do you want from me?" She looked from Trevor back to Del. "Is there even a friend of yours who needs medical help?"

"There is," Trevor answered, drawing her attention back to him. "But it's not the leader of the BRI, sweetheart."

"Then who?"

Trevor nodded toward the cabin. Following his gaze, Nicki saw the front door open and a woman exit, holding the hand of a small boy of four or five. The child was pale and thin, too thin for his gangly height, and dark circles shadowed the skin beneath his eyes.

The woman eyed the men with rifles as she led the child to the edge of the porch. She was a tall, thin woman in her early thirties, but she looked nearly as pale and haggard as her little boy. Her red-rimmed eyes rose and locked with Nicki's, wide with desperation.

"Oh, Trevor," Nicki murmured, her heart squeezing. "Your son?"

"My son," he answered quietly. "So you see, I really don't care who you're working for. Or why. Because now, you're working for me. And you're going to stay here and do whatever you can to get my little boy well."

Chapter Sixteen

The day was unseasonably mild for mid-February in the Blue Ridge Mountains, only a faint breeze adding a hint of chill to the midday sunshine. This deep in the mountains, however, the canopy of evergreen boughs blocked out most of the warming sun, forcing Dallas to hunch more deeply beneath his borrowed camouflage jacket to ward off the cold.

He'd been fortunate that John Bartholomew carried an extra jacket in his truck, and more fortunate still that his feet were only a half size smaller than his benefactor's, the difference in size between his feet and the sturdy dirt-colored hiking boots easily minimized by wearing a second pair of socks. The shirt and pants Nicki had purchased at the thrift store were a little too short in the legs and sleeves, but they fit well enough and kept him reasonably warm as they trekked as silently as possible through the dry underbrush toward the blinking red light that denoted Nicki's position on the GPS map.

The borrowed Smith & Wesson M&P .40 tucked into a holster behind his back felt heavy against his spine, as well. The good kind of heavy, the kind that said he wasn't going into this fight unarmed.

John drew up and held out his arm to block Dallas from walking past him. He turned to look at Dallas, his hazel eyes blending in remarkably with the woodland camouflage face paint he'd smeared over his face before they left the truck and headed into the woods. He nodded his head toward a point directly ahead of them before turning around again.

Dallas peered through the shadowy gloom and spotted what John had seen—the edge of a clearing about seventy yards due east. Movement caught Dallas's eye, but he couldn't make out what he was seeing.

Beside him, John lifted a small pair of binoculars to his eyes and took a look. He held up three fingers.

Three what? Three little pigs? The Three Stooges? What the hell did three fingers mean?

John must have sensed his confusion, for he turned a quick glance his way and murmured, "Three men. Near a cabin. We need to get closer, but you're going to have to move slowly and carefully. And silently. Understood?"

Dallas nodded.

John started picking his way carefully ahead, moving with deliberation and stealth. Dallas fell into his wake, drawing on his own long-forgotten skills in the woods. He'd learned to hunt at a young age, sent out with his brother to bring in food to supplement what his father could steal or purchase with the money his drug sales brought in. He and his brother Clanton had seen themselves as modern-day Daniel Boones, blazing new trails through the mountains of Harlan County, Kentucky.

Of course, those trails had all been blazed long before, by good men and evil men, and his childhood dreams of adventure and discovery had soon given way to the reality of his dead-end existence.

He'd gotten himself out of Kentucky, used his wits and his brains to create a new life for himself. Yet here he was again, creeping through the woods in search of prey.

The human kind, this time.

They closed the distance to just under twenty yards from the sunlit cabin now visible through the thinning trees. John pulled to a halt and crouched behind a scrubby huckleberry bush. Dallas squatted beside him and gazed toward the cabin. The three men John had seen before were still visible, standing near the low-slung front porch. A fourth was now visible, leaning against the railings of the porch steps. Sunlight gleamed on the barrels of the rifles they carried.

John spoke quietly, his voice barely more than a hiss of air in the wind rustling the pine needles overhead. "Remington 798. Browning X-Bolt. Marlin XS7. Another Remington. Model Five, I think."

He was telling Dallas what kind of guns they were up against, as if he felt certain Dallas would know what those guns were and what they could do.

Which suggested John knew a little more about Dallas than most people did. Enough to know that he was more than just some civilian graphic designer working for the FBI. That he might know a little something about rifles.

And, if the trust John had shown so far meant anything, he also believed Dallas knew a little something about moving with stealth through the woods, as well.

Just how much did Alexander Quinn and his people know about him and his past, anyway?

John edged a few yards forward, toward another bush. Dallas followed, wincing as his foot hit a dry twig, making it snap.

For a moment, the nearest man jerked to attention, his brow furrowed. He glanced toward the trees, and Dallas and John both froze in place. Camouflaged as they were, it would be movement that would give them away. Dallas breathed shallowly, keeping his eyes half-closed as he peered toward the alerted rifleman. The man finally appeared to relax and wandered away from the corner of the porch.

After a long pause, John led them forward another few yards and finally hunkered down again. From their new vantage point, they had a decent view of the whole yard in front of the trees.

There was a large blue Chevy pickup truck parked at the edge of the yard. John turned to look at Dallas, a grim smile twisting the corners of his mouth. "Del McClintock," he said quietly.

Dallas took another look at the truck. The cab was empty, so Del and Nicki were apparently inside the cabin.

The very well-guarded cabin.

What were they going to do now?

"I CAN'T SEEM to fix things for Jason. Much as I try." Lynette Colley's pale eyes met Nicki's with wary hope. "Trevor says you can help him."

"I can help with some things," Nicki said as gently as she could manage. Whatever she might think of Trevor and his merry band of thugs, Lynette Colley's love and fear for her child was unmistakable and genuine.

"I know he needs insulin, and Trevor takes care of that, no worries, but ain't there more he needs?" Lynette touched Jason's pale cheek, her expression teeming with concern that made Nicki's heart ache.

"Jason needs a doctor," she said quietly but firmly.

Lynette slanted a look at her. "Trevor ain't gonna have it. You know he ain't. That's why you're here."

"He loves his son, doesn't he?"

"Yes." Lynette's chin came up in a show of angry defiance. "Don't you dare suggest he don't."

"I wouldn't," Nicki said quickly. And she wasn't suggesting any such thing. Clearly, whatever his sins and faults, Trevor Colley loved his son enough to take a woman hostage in order for his son to have the care he needed.

But Nicki wasn't a doctor, and while she'd had some experience helping people with diabetes, her experiences had been more with adults suffering from type 2 diabetes. Type 1 diabetes, the kind that had once been called childhood diabetes, was a whole different animal.

Still, Jason Colley was clearly ill, and there were things she knew how to do to get his blood sugar levels back to a better place on a continuing basis. "We need his glucometer."

Lynette nodded. "You want to test him now?"

At the strangled tone of his mother's voice, Jason looked up with dismay. "No tests, Mama. Okay? No tests."

Nicki crouched next to where the boy sat on the sofa. "Jason, has your mama told you what diabetes is?"

"It's what makes me sick." He sounded more irritated than afraid. "I can't have candy except sometimes."

"It's because things like candy and mashed potatoes and cookies—all those things are full of carbohydrates. Do you know what carbohydrates are?"

He shook his head no.

"They're part of the things that make foods good for you. But in your case, too many of them can make food very bad for you."

He stared at her, clearly not understanding.

"Ever been stung by a bee?"

His eyes widened. "I hate bees."

"Me, too," she said, glancing at Lynette with a smile. "But did you know bees can be good things?"

He looked skeptical.

"They help plants grow," she said, keeping it simple. "When they do that, they're good."

"But not when they sting you," he insisted.

"Definitely not when they sting you." She looked at Lynette with a little nod. Lynette rose and left the room for a moment.

Jason followed his mother's exit with worried eyes, but he looked back at Nicki when she spoke. "Carbohydrates are like bees. When they work the way they're supposed to, they help your body grow like bees help plants grow."

"Until they sting you," he groused.

"Yup, until they sting you."

"Tests sting."

"They do," she agreed. "But they help us know whether or not we need to give you medicine to make you feel better."

Lynette came back in the room with a small pouch. She set the pouch on the coffee table in front of the sofa where Jason sat and looked at Nicki.

Nicki pulled the glucometer from the pouch. It was a medium-sized monitor, not really ideal for the continual level of glucose testing Jason needed if he was going to keep his blood sugar well regulated. Nicki looked up at Lynette. "Where'd you get this?"

The woman looked panic-stricken. "Is it wrong?"

"No," Nicki assured her. "It can do what you need to do. Did a doctor prescribe this?"

Lynette shook her head. "I told you—"

"How'd you get a diagnosis?"

"I got a friend to take us to Bristol a few months ago. I knew somethin' was wrong—"

Nicki pressed her mouth to a thin line. "And Trevor wouldn't let you take him to a doctor?"

Lynette shot her a defensive look. "He has his reasons."

Fear and stupidity, apparently. "The doctor diagnosed him?"

"Yeah. He wanted me to come back, let him see Jason again in a few days, but—"

"But Trevor wouldn't let you." She looked at Jason, who was staring with apprehension at the lancing device sitting next to the glucometer. She looked in one of the inner pockets of the pouch and found a sealed packet containing a few alcohol wipes. She'd already washed her hands before entering the room, but to be safe, she opened an alcohol wipe and gave her hands a quick cleaning before she picked up the lancing device. "How often do you test his blood?" she asked as she cocked the device.

In front of her, Jason made a soft moaning sound.

"He hates it so much, I try not to do it more than twice a day."

"That's not often enough." Nicki shot Lynette an apologetic look. "I know you both don't want to hear that, but regular testing is necessary to keep his blood sugar from reaching dangerous levels."

Tears welled in Lynette's eyes as she gazed at her son. "He hates it so much."

"I bet you hate feeling sick even more, don't you, Jason?"

His gaze snapped up from the lancing device and met hers. "I just want to play with the other kids."

His plaintive reply made her heart hurt. No matter how she'd come to be here, or how much danger she might be in, she was going to help this little boy if she could.

Maybe that was as close to a princess with rainbow-colored wings as she'd ever get, but that would be pretty damn good, wouldn't it?

"Let's see if we can do something about that," she said, turning on the glucometer and holding out her hand to him.

Tentatively, he reached over and laid his hand, palm up, in hers.

She wielded the lancet as gently as she could, but she couldn't make it painless. Jason whimpered a little as the lancet pierced his skin, but he didn't cry. Tough little kid.

She touched the droplet of blood from his finger to the test strip in the glucometer. A few seconds later, the reading came up on the meter. "It's too high," she told Lynette. "When did he last eat?"

"A few hours ago."

"When did you last administer insulin?"

Lynette's face creased with distress. "Last night."

"We need to give him another shot. Now."

Jason started crying. Lynette moved to comfort him, but Nicki caught her arm. "Get the insulin now."

Lynette changed course, and Nicki reached out to put her arms around Jason. He resisted at first, but then he laid his head against her shoulder and started to relax.

The door to the room slammed open and Trevor entered, his usually friendly expression hard as granite. "What are you doing to him?"

She met Trevor's gaze without flinching. "What you brought me here to do. I'm trying to make him feel better."

"You sayin' I want something different?"

She was growing sick of these belligerently ignorant men and their ceaseless bullying. "I'm saying you're too afraid of hospitals and doctors to get your son the help he needs, so I'm all you've got. You need me more than I need you, so stop throwing your weight around as if you can scare me into doing what you want. Because you can't."

His nostrils flared with anger, but he didn't speak.

She'd take that as a win.

Trevor backed out of the room, slamming the door shut behind him. A moment later, the door opened again and Lynette returned, bringing with her a bag of supplies.

"Did he yell at you?" she asked quietly as she handed the bag to Nicki.

"Not much," she answered with a smile of reassurance as she retrieved the insulin and syringes from the bag. "Did the doctor you saw in Bristol prescribe the dosage written on this package?"

"Yes, but we're nearly out."

Of course they were. She kept her mouth firmly shut and opened one of the syringes, earning another soft whimper from Jason. She tamped down the rush of sympathy, knowing what the little boy needed from her now was competence, not sentiment.

"You've been giving him the shots in the soft part of his belly, right?"

"Yes."

"Think you can help me out, Jason?" she asked, turning to the boy. He gazed back at her, wide-eyed. "Do you know how to pinch someone?"

His eyes widened even more. "Mama says I'm not s'posed to pinch."

"Well, sometimes it's okay. Like now." She held out her arm. "Pinch me. Right here on my arm."

He hesitated for a moment, glancing at his mother. She gave a nod, and he turned back to Nicki, reached out and pinched her arm.

"Ow!" she cried, making him jerk back from her. Then she grinned. "Just kidding. That barely hurt at all."

Slowly, he grinned, showing his teeth for the first time. "You tricked me."

"I did," she agreed. "Now, can you pinch your tummy just like you pinched my arm?"

Frowning, he looked down at his T-shirt. "Why?"

"Because if you're pinching your belly when I give you the shot, you might not even feel the shot. Want to give it a try?"

He hesitated a moment, then tugged his shirt up, baring his belly. She saw a couple of little bruises that had probably come from previous injections. He pinched a little bit of the flesh just below his navel.

"Can you feel the pinch?" she asked.

He nodded, squeezing a little harder.

"Close your eyes now and just pinch."

He did as she asked, and she quickly injected the insulin into the pinched skin. "All done."

He opened his eyes and looked at her. "You're tricking me again."

"Nope, all done."

Behind her, Lynette started to cry.

THE MEN WITH the rifles left, one at a time, until by just before nightfall, only the Silverado remained parked in front of the cabin. Hours of stillness had begun to make Dallas's legs and arms ache, reminding him that however improved he might be since his escape from captivity, he was still recuperating.

This wasn't the place where he'd been held captive. He was certain of that. But he was pretty sure it had been somewhere close by. The terrain was right. The lay of the land. And after a few minutes of surveillance, he was certain that at least one of the armed men guarding the cabin had been among those who'd kept guard over him while he was in the BRI's custody.

The fact that he'd managed to realize that bit of information without giving in to emotional paralysis was a victory of sorts. He was still plagued with nightmares, and probably would be for a while yet, but in the cold light of day, he wasn't going to be held hostage by those memories.

"Closest side window," John murmured, the first words he'd spoken in well over an hour.

Dallas followed his gaze and saw the curtains shift in the window closest to the corner of the cabin. A face appeared there briefly, lit by the setting rays of the sun.

Nicki's face.

So she was in there. The GPS signal had suggested as much, of course, but now they had visual confirmation.

Was she a prisoner? Or was she still playing her part?

"How sure is Quinn that they know she's undercover?" he asked John.

"He wouldn't have sent us after her if he wasn't sure."

Dallas looked at the window again. She'd disappeared from the space between the curtains, replaced by a tall, broad-shouldered man who peered out at the woods with a frown on his face.

"Del McClintock," John said.

Dallas took another look at the man before, like Nicki, he'd backed away from the window and disappeared from view. "If they know she's an undercover operative, why haven't they finished her off?" Merely saying the words aloud made his stomach ache. "They don't even seem to be keeping her prisoner, do they?"

"If you mean she's not shackled in a cellar

somewhere, no they don't." John's voice softened. "But there are many ways to be kept captive."

Dallas looked at the cabin, his gaze settling on the window where he'd last seen Nicki's face.

"I know," he said.

That's what scared him.

Chapter Seventeen

"I didn't know they were going to do this to you."

Lynette Colley's soft voice roused Nicki from a half doze. She sat up straight and looked up to find the other woman now sitting in the rocking chair across from her, holding her sleeping child.

Jason's blood sugar had finally reached a normal level and was so far maintaining, even after a light dinner. He'd fallen asleep soon after, exhausted from the illness and the trauma of the day.

Nicki knew just how he felt.

"How long have you been here?" she asked, stifling a yawn.

"Just a few minutes. The men just finished eating."

Nicki glanced around the room, making certain they were alone. She lowered her voice a notch. "Who's here now?"

"Del and Trevor. The others left before I made

dinner. I don't think they're coming back until morning."

Nicki got up and looked out the window. Outside, night had fallen, only the faintest of indigo still touching the sky to the west. "Is this cabin usually guarded like this?"

"No," Lynette answered, sounding as tired as she looked. "When I married him, Trevor was just a short-order cook. We were poor, I suppose, but happy. And then I found out I was pregnant. Things got more complicated."

"Poor and happy wasn't enough?"

"I guess not." She sighed. "You take shortcuts. Then it works and you start to get some of the things you never had, and you end up wanting more and more. No matter how much you get, it just ain't enough. I swear these hills are hell on earth. And I guess that means Trevor's become the devil himself now. 'Cause he's the king around these parts."

"I'm from the hills," Nicki murmured, turning back to look at Lynette. "Sometimes, I look at places like this, with all the wildness and the beauty, and I wonder how anything bad could ever come from a place this grand."

"You think I'm a terrible mama, don't you?"

"I think you love your son. And you're scared. And you don't know how to give him what he needs." She crossed to the rocking chair and crouched in front of Lynette, thinking about Kaylie Pickett and that little baby still holding on inside her despite all the odds against him. These hills could be harsh and unforgiving, but grace could still be found. Courage.

Miracles.

What she was about to say could get her killed, she knew. But it could also save three lives.

"Lynette, if I could get you and Jason out of here, I could help you get everything you need to give him as normal a life as possible. I can see that's what you want for him."

Tears welled in Lynette's eyes. "Trevor wouldn't let me take him out of here."

"If that's true, then we have to take him out of here without Trevor knowing."

The thought caused Lynette real pain, Nicki saw. Whatever his flaws and his sins, Trevor meant something strong and binding to his wife. Leaving him would break her heart.

But if she didn't leave him, she might lose her son.

Damn Trevor. Damn him for putting this woman in the position to have to choose.

"You helped him before. Can't you keep helping him?" Lynette gazed at her sleeping son, tears dripping from her eyes and landing on his cheek. He stirred in his sleep, lifting one hand to wipe away his mother's tears.

"Not long-term. He needs close monitoring and frequent doctor's visits."

"I can't afford that. You know I can't."

"There are programs that can help you. People who would help you."

Lynette looked up. "Like you, I suppose?"

"I would."

She shook her head. "If we get out of here, you're gonna press charges against Trevor."

"If we escape, I don't know that anyone will be able to track down Trevor for a long, long time." She knew he wouldn't stick around to face the law. One thing the members of the Blue Ridge Infantry had gotten very good at was disappearing when the heat was on.

Lynette's face crumpled. "I know you can't understand this, but I do love him."

Nicki put her hand over Lynette's. "I do understand. I know what it's like to love someone difficult."

"Are you in love with Del?" Lynette asked.

Nicki's gaze snapped up to meet hers. "No."

"But you have a man, don't you?" Lynette's mouth curved a little, the expression driving away some of the haggard lines from her facing, hinting at the pretty young woman she must have been when Trevor Colley made her his bride. "A woman as pretty as you are. Is he difficult, too?"

An image of Dallas's face flashed through her

mind, and she felt the keen ache of longing. What must he be thinking right now? She should have been home ages ago. Was he starting to panic? Had he already used her phone to call for help?

What if he tried to find her? It would be just like him to put his neck on the line for her that way, wouldn't it?

But he would be outnumbered. Even if he was in top fighting form—and she knew he wasn't, despite his remarkable improvement over the past few days—he was still at a severe disadvantage. It would be one unarmed man fighting at least two armed men just to get anywhere near this cabin.

"He's very difficult," she admitted aloud. "Stubborn and impossible."

But, somehow, she loved him, anyway.

Oh, God, she thought. *I love him?*

She almost laughed at the sheer absurdity of her bad timing.

"Could you leave him?"

"I left him to come here." She looked at Jason's sleep-softened features and felt her heart squeeze into a knot. "I knew I might never see him again if I took this job. But it was the right thing to do." She looked up at Lynette. "Jason will never have a normal life here. Trevor will never do what it takes to make that happen. You know that, don't you?"

Lynette's lip trembled, but finally she nodded.

"Is there a way out of here without going past Del and Trevor?"

Lynette stared at her a long moment. "We don't have to worry about Del and Trevor."

Nicki met her gaze, confused. "Why not?"

Lynette kissed the top of her son's head and smiled a faint smile. "Because I put enough diazepam in the beef stew I served for dinner to keep them asleep at least a couple of hours."

THERE WAS NO way of knowing how many people were inside the cabin, though over the past hour, Dallas had seen a second man looking out one of the front windows and what had looked like the silhouette of a woman in the same window where he'd earlier seen Nicki. "It's not Nicki," he'd told John confidently. Nicki was taller and curvier than the slim woman whose shadow had passed by the window.

"I think the second man we saw may be Trevor Colley," John murmured. "Nicki's boss at the diner."

Dallas frowned. "She never mentioned he was connected to the BRI."

"Maybe she didn't know."

"Did Quinn?"

John's face turned toward him, his eyes glinting in the dark. "If Quinn had known, he'd have told her."

"Come on. Quinn was a former spook. You think you can trust a former spook to tell you everything you need to know?"

For a second, John's teeth gleamed in the low light.

Well, hell, Dallas thought. "You're a former spook, too, aren't you?"

"Not for nearly as long as Quinn," John answered, still grinning.

Dallas supposed it was probably a good thing that John knew a few sneaky spy tricks, but on the whole, he'd have preferred to have a few extra men on his team. Well-armed men who knew how to take and hold ground in a fight.

He had to believe Nicki was still all right. Any other option was unthinkable.

Unbearable.

She was the most remarkable woman he'd ever met, a combination of sweetness and fire. Strength and gentleness. Compassion and steel. He had no idea if he deserved a chance to make her his woman, no idea if he was worthy of being her man, but he damned well intended to find out.

Which meant he had to figure out a way to get her out of that cabin to safety.

"I think we're down to just two men, a woman and Nicki," he said quietly. "They're armed, but so are we."

"They probably have multiple weapons at their disposal," John warned.

Dallas nodded. "But we have surprise."

John slanted another curious look his way. "You have something in mind, don't you?"

"This isn't the place where they kept me when I was their prisoner before. But it's a lot like it."

"So?"

"So, maybe this cabin also has an underground cellar where they keep prisoners now and then."

"You think that's where Nicki's being kept?"

"Maybe. Or maybe, if it's like the one where they had me chained up before, it has both an outside and an inside access point."

"You mean if we could find the outside door to the cellar, it might give us a way to get inside the house."

Dallas nodded. "Exactly."

"They'll hear the door opening."

"Unless they're busy doing something else. Like, say, checking out the distraction going on at the front of the cabin."

John's eyes narrowed. "I'm guessing I'd be the distraction?"

Dallas shrugged one shoulder. "Nicki knows what I look like. She doesn't know you. She might not trust you at first, and that would slow everything up too much."

The other man's lips flattened, but he nodded

for Dallas to follow him toward the back of the cabin. "So let's find out if that cellar exists."

The grass was high behind the cabin, dry from the winter but overgrown, as if they'd not bothered to mow it down after the summer growth. With spring just around the corner, the danger of stirring up hibernating snakes in that overgrowth hovered at the back of Dallas's mind as he edged out into the open, staying low to the ground and moving slowly through the grass in search of—

He almost tripped over the door set into the ground near the back edge of the clearing. Dead leaves hid most of the wood-slat door from view, but the hasp that held it closed glinted in the wisps of moonlight visible through the clouds scudding across the night sky.

There was a padlock looped through the hasp closure, which would keep it from opening easily from inside. But the lock itself wasn't engaged. As quietly as he could, Dallas unthreaded the padlock from the hasp and laid it aside in the high grass.

He looked up to find John Bartholomew watching him from a few yards away, his eyes barely visible over the waist-high grass. Dallas gave a nod, flashing a brief smile of triumph.

John's nostrils flared for a moment, then he edged over to where Dallas crouched. "Get in there, make sure the cellar is clear and see if there's a door to the inside. Then come back and report."

Dallas stared at the other man for a long moment, realizing how easy it would be for John to double-cross him if that was his intention. Once Dallas was inside the cellar, John could simply put the lock in the hasp and shut it. Or jab a sturdy stick in the hasp to keep it closed for that matter.

Of course, if John had wanted to double-cross him, he could have shot him dead at any point on this crazy search for Nicki, couldn't he?

He had to trust someone. Nicki's life was at stake, and no matter how much he might wish things were different, this was one rescue mission he couldn't pull off by himself.

Taking a deep breath, he opened the cellar door, wincing as the hinges creaked a little. Hopefully, the sound hadn't carried inside the cabin.

"Cover my back," he whispered and eased himself onto the stairs barely visible through the open doorway.

"Take this," John said, holding something out to him. It was a key chain, Dallas saw, with a small flashlight attached. He closed his hands around the keys to keep them from rattling and nodded his thanks, then headed down the steps.

The cellar was pitch-black and musty smelling once he got to the bottom. He listened a minute for any sound of habitation. There was the faint scuttle of something small and probably rodent somewhere within the cellar's dank confines. He turned on the flashlight, hoping whatever he'd heard had already scurried out of sight.

The cellar was smaller than he'd anticipated. He felt the first smothering sensation of claustrophobia, a sensation that only intensified when the flashlight beam swept over a set of shackles bolted to the wall.

A flood of dark memories nearly paralyzed him, but he forced himself to breathe deeply and slowly, concentrating on keeping his pulse steady. After a moment, the dizzying slideshow in his mind faded away and he moved forward into the cellar.

There was a steep set of steps at the other end of the room, leading up to a door at the top. He tested the first step carefully. It was sturdier than he'd anticipated, not even creaking beneath his weight.

He eased up the stairs until he reached the top. With great care, he tried the door handle. It turned in his hand, unlocked.

Okay. Okay, then.

He backed down the steps and crossed to the outdoor hatch, gazing up at John's face peering over the edge. "The inside door is unlocked. Give me a diversion in two minutes and I'll get in there and get Nicki out."

John gave a short nod and moved out of sight.

Dallas retraced his steps to the top of the other set of stairs, willing himself to remain calm.

LYNETTE CAME BACK into the room, her eyes bright with a blend of fear and excitement. "They're both asleep. But we gotta be real quiet. They're not unconscious. Just sedated."

Nicki nodded, tucking Jason more snugly in her arms. "Is there a back door?"

"Yeah, but it creaks real loud when you open it. That could wake one of 'em."

Damn it. "We can't go out past them, can we?"

"There's the cellar," Lynette suggested, nodding for Nicki to follow her. "It has an outside exit."

Praying the movement wouldn't wake the sleeping little boy, Nicki shifted his weight to one hip as she followed Lynette into the darkened hallway. To the left, she saw dim lamplight filtering into the hall from the front room where Del and Trevor were dozing. To the right, there was a closed door.

They reached the door and Lynette started to reach for the knob when there were two sharp cracks of noise coming from the front of the house. Lynette's body jerked, bumping into Nicki and jostling Jason awake.

"Mama?" he cried.

Down the hall, Nicki heard the sound of stumbling footsteps.

"Go!" she growled, pushing Lynette toward the door.

But before either of them could touch the knob, the door swung open, nearly hitting them. Lynette fell back, bumping Nicki into the wall as a man's broad shoulders filled the narrow opening.

Dark, familiar eyes locked with hers. Her heart skipped a beat.

Then Dallas grabbed her. "Let's get out of here."

THE VOLLEY OF fire coming from the front porch might have seemed as if it was coming from a small army, but there appeared to be only two armed men defending the cabin.

John pinned them down with a couple of shots from his own pistol, observing them carefully enough to notice they were moving sluggishly, their reactions slow and largely inaccurate.

But even bad marksmen got lucky now and then. One of the wildly aimed shots pinged off the tailgate of the Silverado parked in the yard and sliced a deep furrow through the top of John's shoulder. The fiery pain that quickly followed seemed accompanied by an odd numbness in the arm below it. Not his weapon hand, thank God, but for all intents and purposes, his left arm was currently useless.

He fired more shots and shifted to a new position before they could fire back, trying to angle his way toward the back of the house, where he hoped Dallas and Nicki would be emerging from the cellar at any moment.

Then shots fired from the woods behind him threw his plan into utter disarray.

"WHO ARE YOU?" The slender woman standing between him and Nicki stared at him in shock, flinching each time a gunshot sounded behind her.

"He's a friend," Nicki said, pushing Lynette forward with one hand while holding the crying little boy tightly despite his frantic squirming. "Lynette, take him." She pushed the child into the other woman's arms and looked at Dallas. "Are you okay?"

As the woman she'd called Lynette gathered the crying child into her arms, Dallas caught Nicki's hand, the warm solidity of her skin pressed to his nothing less than a lifeline. He didn't know who this woman and child were, but it was enough that Nicki was trying to help them. That made them his responsibility, as well.

While the sound of gunfire at the front of the

cabin seemed to have Lynette's nerves stretched to the breaking point, Dallas took heart from it. It meant John was keeping the other men occupied, at least for the time being. He went up the steps first, then reached back down to help Lynette and the boy climb out of the cellar. Nicki brought up the rear, gazing at him with eyes that looked as shiny and pale as the peekaboo moon.

"Who's doing the shooting?" she asked in a low tone as she let go of his hand.

"You know him as Agent X."

A rattling noise in the dry grass nearby startled Dallas into a crouch. He grabbed the pistol from the holster at his back, looking for the source of the sound. Suddenly John Bartholomew's head rose over the top of the grass, his gaze meeting Dallas's.

"More men coming. I'm going to lead them away. Get them out of here. Use the truck. Don't wait for me."

There was something odd about the way John was holding himself, as if one half of his torso was sagging lower than the other, but Dallas didn't have time to make out any more details before John turned and scurried toward the woods on the other side of the house.

Dallas heard gunfire erupt on that side of the house and realized he had to be on the move.

Now.

He grabbed Nicki's elbow and pushed her toward the woods in the opposite direction, away from where John seemed to be leading their pursuers.

Ahead of them, Lynette was running with more speed than he'd expected a thin, fragile-looking woman her size would be able to muster up, especially burdened with a child on her hip. Dallas glanced at Nicki as they started to race after her. "Watch our backs," he said, picking up speed to catch up with Lynette.

"Always," Nicki called softly after him, her words carried on the cool night breeze.

"Follow me," Dallas murmured to Lynette as he passed her, leading the way through the woods to where John had parked the truck. He knew there would be no time, no chance to wait for John to reach them. He'd told them not to wait, and as much as it went against Dallas's instincts to leave the man behind, he knew he had no choice.

The truck was where they'd left it, just far enough off the shoulder to be hidden from easy view from the road. Dallas unlocked the back door of the extended cab and helped Lynette onto the narrow bench seat. "Buckle him in and try to stay low," he told her as he unlocked the door for Nicki.

By the time he'd reached the driver's door, Nicki had already unlocked it for him, holding out her hand to help him climb in. Not bothering with seat belts for the moment, he started the truck and pulled out onto the empty road, bracing for the worst.

But no gunfire followed them. No armed trucks pulled out in pursuit to run them off the road the way Dallas had been run off the road the last time he'd met up with the BRI.

In fact, for four or five miles, they saw no sign of any other vehicles at all. The emptiness of the road ahead, illuminated by the truck's headlights, evoked an eerie feeling of isolation in the pit of Dallas's stomach, as if the four of them had escaped an apocalyptic disaster only to find themselves the last people left on a desolated earth.

When he first heard the engine noise, it was almost a relief. Until he realized it was moving closer—and louder—at an impossible rate of speed. As it neared, the sound became more distinct, the heavy *whump-whump* of spinning rotor blades unmistakable.

The noise became deafening and then the helicopter came into view, impossibly close to the ground, and settled about three hundred yards down the highway in front of them.

Dallas just had time to bring the truck to a stop

short of the whipping rotors. He turned to look at Nicki. She met his gaze, her eyes wide and afraid.

The sudden appearance of the helicopter had at least stunned the crying child into silence, Dallas thought as he glanced back to see both mother and child staring at the spectacle through the windshield with slack mouths and startled eyes.

Movement in the periphery of his vision caught his attention, and he peered through the windshield to see a man illuminated in the truck's headlights. He was bent low, beneath the downdraft of the spinning helicopter rotors, but Dallas could make out a head full of sandy brown hair and the faint shadow of a goatee covering the man's chin.

Beside him, Nicki started to laugh. He looked at her, wondering if the stress of the day had finally gotten to her.

She grinned at him, nodding toward the man approaching the truck.

"That," she said, "is how Alexander Quinn makes an entrance."

Epilogue

"We haven't located John Bartholomew yet."

Nicki opened her gritty eyes and saw Alexander Quinn standing in front of her, holding out a steaming cup of coffee.

"Which means you haven't found his body, either," she said, wishing she felt as optimistic as her words would suggest. But she'd seen enough battles in the war between the Blue Ridge Infantry and their enemies to know that the lack of a body didn't always mean a death hadn't occurred.

"If he's alive, he'll find a way to get in touch." Quinn sat on the edge of his desk in front of her, nodding toward the door to the hallway. "I think they're nearly done with Cole."

"They" were a small group of US congressmen who'd agreed to meet with Dallas on neutral ground, which was how Quinn described the conference room at The Gates. The security firm's offices were located in a slightly shabby old Victorian house in the heart of Purgatory, Tennessee, as unlikely a setting for a high-powered security firm as Nicki could imagine.

Nicki herself had undergone questioning by the FBI soon after she arrived in Purgatory, but somehow Quinn had managed to keep the feds away from Dallas until he could set up the meeting with the congressmen who were looking into the troubling suicide of an FBI assistant director named Philip Crandall.

"They're not sure it's suicide," Quinn had confided to Nicki when he told her about Crandall's death.

"What do you think?"

He'd shrugged. "It could go either way."

She pushed up from the chair, stretching her legs. She slept the past two nights at the office, in one of the six dormitory rooms housed in what used to be the mansion's basement. She had no idea where Dallas had spent those nights, as Quinn had separated them the minute the helicopter touched down on the helipad they'd constructed atop the hardware store down the street, much to the chagrin of Nicki's cousin Anson and his wife Ginny, who lived in the loft apartment just below the new helipad.

Anson and Ginny had greeted her warmly, reminding her that no matter how alone she sometimes felt, she wasn't without people who cared about her. She had Anson and Ginny.

She hoped she had Dallas as well, but it would be nice to finally get to talk to him.

"I know you can't tell me where Lynette and Jason are, but have you heard anything from them? Is Jason okay?"

Quinn's features softened, just a notch. "They're both fine. The doctors treating Jason believe he will respond well to regular treatment, and they're making sure Lynette knows how to help provide it."

"And Trevor can't get to them?"

A strange look came over Quinn's face.

"What is it?" Nicki asked.

"Trevor is dead."

Nicki sat again, the news catching her by surprise. "How?"

"The investigators believe Del McClintock shot him, then fled."

She pressed her hand to her lips, remembering the man she'd worked with for a couple of months. The man whose secret life had caught her completely flat-footed.

"Does Lynette know?"

"Yes."

The door to the office opened. Nicki looked up and saw Dallas standing in the doorway, looking thinner than she remembered. Older.

But alive. Gloriously alive and gazing back at her with fire in his dark eyes.

"I'll go speak with the congressmen," Quinn said as Nicki rose to her feet, her gaze following Dallas all the way in as he crossed to where they stood. Quinn nodded and left his office, closing the door behind him.

For a moment, Dallas just looked at her, his gaze seeming to drink her in. She let her own gaze roam over him, taking stock of the small changes their brief time apart had wrought. He hadn't shaved, his beard dark on his jaw and chin. Her first assessment was right—he looked thinner, giving his features a lean, almost feral appearance.

But his eyes were clear and bright, full of an emotion she was afraid to believe. "Are you okay?" he asked.

She almost laughed. "I'm fine. How are you?"

"Tired," he admitted. "Wrung out."

She couldn't stop herself from reaching out to touch him, her fingers rasping on his beard stubble and settling against the side of his neck. "What happens next?" At his slightly puzzled look, she added, "With the congressmen. Do you have to deal with the FBI next?"

"No," he answered quickly. "The FBI is satisfied with my story. Apparently your boss has a great deal of influence within certain agencies of the government. But I'm not going to be able to resume my job with the Bureau."

She hadn't thought he would. "So you're a free agent, then."

"An unemployed free agent."

"Quinn's always looking for smart people. You're smart."

"I'm a graphic designer."

"Who was studying to be a cybersecurity expert."

"Who wasn't finished studying yet."

"We can work on that," she said firmly, stroking his collarbone with her thumb.

His lips curved in a smile. "We?"

She took a step closer, shivering a little when his hands settled over the curve of her hips. "I thought we made a pretty good team. Didn't you?"

He lowered his head until his forehead touched hers. "I did, actually."

"You don't just break up a good team if you don't have to."

He nuzzled his nose against hers, sparking another delicious shiver down her spine. "No, you really don't."

"So we're agreed?"

He drew his head back, looking down at her through slightly narrowed eyes. "Agreed?"

A flutter of alarm darted through her belly. "That we're a team."

"Depends."

"Depends?"

He bent closer again, his lips brushing against the curve of her earlobe. "Do teammates get to kiss?" he whispered.

She turned her head to whisper back. "Among other things."

He pulled back just enough to grin at her. "Never let it be said I'm not a team player." Then he bent and pressed his lips to hers.

She tugged him closer, relishing the feel of his heartbeat thudding a lively cadence against her breast as his kiss deepened, his tongue sliding over hers, claiming her. Cherishing her.

Damned if she didn't suddenly feel like a princess.

Rainbow wings and all.

* * * * *

*Don't miss the final installment of
Paula Graves's miniseries*
THE GATES: MOST WANTED
*when STRANGER IN COLD CREEK
goes on sale next month. Look for it wherever
Harlequin Intrigue books and ebooks are sold!*

LARGER-PRINT BOOKS!

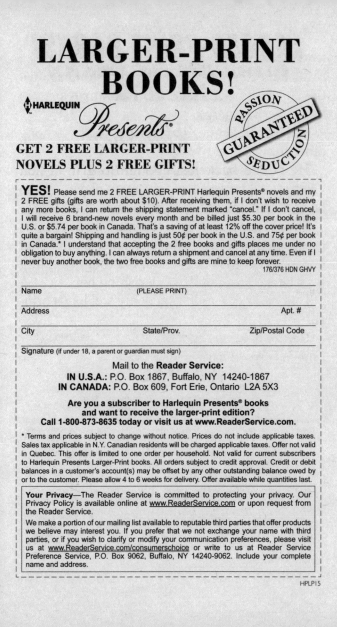

HARLEQUIN

Presents®

PASSION GUARANTEED SEDUCTION

GET 2 FREE LARGER-PRINT NOVELS PLUS 2 FREE GIFTS!

YES! Please send me 2 FREE LARGER-PRINT Harlequin Presents® novels and my 2 FREE gifts (gifts are worth about $10). After receiving them, if I don't wish to receive any more books, I can return the shipping statement marked "cancel." If I don't cancel, I will receive 6 brand-new novels every month and be billed just $5.30 per book in the U.S. or $5.74 per book in Canada. That's a saving of at least 12% off the cover price! It's quite a bargain! Shipping and handling is just 50¢ per book in the U.S. and 75¢ per book in Canada.* I understand that accepting the 2 free books and gifts places me under no obligation to buy anything. I can always return a shipment and cancel at any time. Even if I never buy another book, the two free books and gifts are mine to keep forever.

176/376 HDN GHVY

Name _____ (PLEASE PRINT)

Address _____ Apt. #

City _____ State/Prov. _____ Zip/Postal Code

Signature (if under 18, a parent or guardian must sign)

Mail to the **Reader Service:**
IN U.S.A.: P.O. Box 1867, Buffalo, NY 14240-1867
IN CANADA: P.O. Box 609, Fort Erie, Ontario L2A 5X3

**Are you a subscriber to Harlequin Presents® books
and want to receive the larger-print edition?
Call 1-800-873-8635 today or visit us at www.ReaderService.com.**

* Terms and prices subject to change without notice. Prices do not include applicable taxes. Sales tax applicable in N.Y. Canadian residents will be charged applicable taxes. Offer not valid in Quebec. This offer is limited to one order per household. Not valid for current subscribers to Harlequin Presents Larger-Print books. All orders subject to credit approval. Credit or debit balances in a customer's account(s) may be offset by any other outstanding balance owed by or to the customer. Please allow 4 to 6 weeks for delivery. Offer available while quantities last.

Your Privacy—The Reader Service is committed to protecting your privacy. Our Privacy Policy is available online at www.ReaderService.com or upon request from the Reader Service.

We make a portion of our mailing list available to reputable third parties that offer products we believe may interest you. If you prefer that we not exchange your name with third parties, or if you wish to clarify or modify your communication preferences, please visit us at www.ReaderService.com/consumerschoice or write to us at Reader Service Preference Service, P.O. Box 9062, Buffalo, NY 14240-9062. Include your complete name and address.

HPLP15

LARGER-PRINT BOOKS!

GET 2 FREE LARGER-PRINT NOVELS PLUS
2 FREE GIFTS!

◆ HARLEQUIN®

Romance

From the Heart, For the Heart

YES! Please send me 2 FREE LARGER-PRINT Harlequin® Romance novels and my 2 FREE gifts (gifts are worth about $10). After receiving them, if I don't wish to receive any more books, I can return the shipping statement marked "cancel." If I don't cancel, I will receive 4 brand-new novels every month and be billed just $5.09 per book in the U.S. or $5.49 per book in Canada. That's a savings of at least 15% off the cover price! It's quite a bargain! Shipping and handling is just 50¢ per book in the U.S. and 75¢ per book in Canada.* I understand that accepting the 2 free books and gifts places me under no obligation to buy anything. I can always return a shipment and cancel at any time. Even if I never buy another book, the two free books and gifts are mine to keep forever.

119/319 HDN GHWC

Name	(PLEASE PRINT)

Address	Apt. #

City	State/Prov.	Zip/Postal Code

Signature (if under 18, a parent or guardian must sign)

Mail to the **Reader Service:**
IN U.S.A.: P.O. Box 1867, Buffalo, NY 14240-1867
IN CANADA: P.O. Box 609, Fort Erie, Ontario L2A 5X3

Want to try two free books from another line?
Call 1-800-873-8635 or visit www.ReaderService.com.

* Terms and prices subject to change without notice. Prices do not include applicable taxes. Sales tax applicable in N.Y. Canadian residents will be charged applicable taxes. Offer not valid in Quebec. This offer is limited to one order per household. Not valid for current subscribers to Harlequin Romance Larger-Print books. All orders subject to credit approval. Credit or debit balances in a customer's account(s) may be offset by any other outstanding balance owed by or to the customer. Please allow 4 to 6 weeks for delivery. Offer available while quantities last.

Your Privacy—The Reader Service is committed to protecting your privacy. Our Privacy Policy is available online at www.ReaderService.com or upon request from the Reader Service.

We make a portion of our mailing list available to reputable third parties that offer products we believe may interest you. If you prefer that we not exchange your name with third parties, or if you wish to clarify or modify your communication preferences, please visit us at www.ReaderService.com/consumerchoice or write to us at Reader Service Preference Service, P.O. Box 9062, Buffalo, NY 14240-9062. Include your complete name and address.

HRLP15

LARGER-PRINT BOOKS!
GET 2 FREE LARGER-PRINT NOVELS PLUS
2 FREE GIFTS!

HARLEQUIN®

super romance®

More Story...More Romance

YES! Please send me 2 FREE LARGER-PRINT Harlequin® Superromance® novels and my 2 FREE gifts (gifts are worth about $10). After receiving them, if I don't wish to receive any more books, I can return the shipping statement marked "cancel." If I don't cancel, I will receive 4 brand-new novels every month and be billed just $5.94 per book in the U.S. or $6.24 per book in Canada. That's a savings of at least 12% off the cover price! It's quite a bargain! Shipping and handling is just 50¢ per book in the U.S. or 75¢ per book in Canada.* I understand that accepting the 2 free books and gifts places me under no obligation to buy anything. I can always return a shipment and cancel at any time. Even if I never buy another book, the two free books and gifts are mine to keep forever.

132/332 HDN GHVC

Name _____ (PLEASE PRINT) _____

Address _____ Apt. # _____

City _____ State/Prov. _____ Zip/Postal Code _____

Signature (if under 18, a parent or guardian must sign) _____

Mail to the **Reader Service:**

IN U.S.A.: P.O. Box 1867, Buffalo, NY 14240-1867
IN CANADA: P.O. Box 609, Fort Erie, Ontario L2A 5X3

Want to try two free books from another line?
Call 1-800-873-8635 today or visit www.ReaderService.com.

* Terms and prices subject to change without notice. Prices do not include applicable taxes. Sales tax applicable in N.Y. Canadian residents will be charged applicable taxes. Offer not valid in Quebec. This offer is limited to one order per household. Not valid for current subscribers to Harlequin Superromance Larger-Print books. All orders subject to credit approval. Credit or debit balances in a customer's account(s) may be offset by any other outstanding balance owed by or to the customer. Please allow 4 to 6 weeks for delivery. Offer available while quantities last.

Your Privacy—The Reader Service is committed to protecting your privacy. Our Privacy Policy is available online at www.ReaderService.com or upon request from the Reader Service.

We make a portion of our mailing list available to reputable third parties that offer products we believe may interest you. If you prefer that we not exchange your name with third parties, or if you wish to clarify or modify your communication preferences, please visit us at www.ReaderService.com/consumerschoice or write to us at Reader Service Preference Service, P.O. Box 9062, Buffalo, NY 14240-9062. Include your complete name and address.

HSRLP15

YES! Please send me **The Montana Mavericks Collection** in Larger Print. This collection begins with 3 FREE books and 2 FREE gifts (gifts valued at approx. $20.00 retail) in the first shipment, along with the other first 4 books from the collection! If I do not cancel, I will receive 8 monthly shipments until I have the entire 51-book Montana Mavericks collection. I will receive 2 or 3 FREE books in each shipment and I will pay just $4.99 US/ $5.89 CDN for each of the other four books in each shipment, plus $2.99 for shipping and handling per shipment.*If I decide to keep the entire collection, I'll have paid for only 32 books, because 19 books are FREE! I understand that accepting the 3 free books and gifts places me under no obligation to buy anything. I can always return a shipment and cancel at any time. My free books and gifts are mine to keep no matter what I decide.

263 HCN 2404   463 HCN 2404

Name _____ (PLEASE PRINT) _____

Address _____ Apt. # _____

City _____ State/Prov. _____ Zip/Postal Code _____

Signature (if under 18, a parent or guardian must sign) _____

Mail to the **Reader Service:**

IN U.S.A.: P.O. Box 1867, Buffalo, NY 14240-1867
IN CANADA: P.O. Box 609, Fort Erie, Ontario L2A 5X3